WYATT'S WAR

HEARTS & HEROES
BOOK 1

New York Times & USA Today
Bestselling Author

ELLE JAMES

Dedication

This book is dedicated to the men and women of the armed forces who protect our lives and liberty. I have nothing but love and respect for them and the sacrifices they make daily. Also, I'd like to dedicate this book to their families who keep the home fires burning for their heroes' return.

Chapter One

Sergeant Major Wyatt Magnus pushed past the pain in his knee, forcing himself to finish a three-mile run in the sticky heat of south Texas. Thankfully his ribs had healed and his broken fingers had mended enough he could pull the trigger again. He didn't anticipate needing to use the nine-millimeter Beretta tucked beneath his fluorescent vest. San Antonio wasn't what he'd call a hot zone. Not like Somalia, his last *real* assignment.

It wouldn't be long before his commander saw he was fit for combat duty, not playing the role of a babysitter for fat tourists, politicians and businessmen visiting the Alamo and stuffing themselves on Tex-Mex food while pretending to attend an International Trade Convention.

The scents of fajitas and salsa filled the air, accompanied by the happy cadence of a mariachi band. Twinkle lights lit the trees along the downtown River Walk as he completed his run around the San Antonio Convention Center and started back to his hotel. Neither the food, nor the music lightened his spirits.

Since being medevaced out of Somalia to San Antonio Medical Center, the combined armed forces' medical facility, he'd been chomping at the bit to get back to where the action was. But for some damn reason, his commander and the psych evaluator thought he needed to cool his heels a little longer and get his head on straight before he went back into the more volatile situations.

So what? He'd been captured and tortured by Somali militants. If he hadn't been so trusting of the men he'd been sent to train in combat techniques, he might have picked up on the signs. Staff Sergeant Dane might not be dead and Wyatt wouldn't have spent three of the worst weeks of his life held captive. He'd been tortured: nine fingers, four ribs and one kneecap broken and had been beaten to within an inch of his life. All his training, his experience in the field, the culture briefings and in-country observations hadn't prepared him for complete betrayal by the very people he had been sent there to help.

He understood why the Somali armed forces had turned him over to the residual al-Shabab militants that were attempting a comeback after being ousted from the capital, Mogadishu. He might have done the same if his family had been kidnapped and threatened with torture and beheading if he didn't hand over the foreigners.

No, he'd have found a better way to deal with the terrorists. A way that involved very painful deaths. His breathing grew shallower and the beginning of a panic attack snuck up on him like a freight train.

Focus. The psych doc had given him methods to cope with the onset of anxiety that made him feel like he was having a heart attack. He had to focus to get his mind out of Somalia and torture and back to San Antonio and the River Walk.

Ahead he spied the pert twitch of a female butt encased in hot pink running shorts and a neon green tank top. Her ass was as far from the dry terrain of Somalia as a guy could get. Wyatt focused on her and her tight buttocks, picking up the pace to catch up. She was a pretty young woman with an MP3 device strapped to her arm with wires leading to the earbuds in her ears. Her dark red hair pulled back in a loose ponytail bounced with every step. Running in *the zone*, she seemed to ignore everything around but the path in front of her.

Once he caught up, Wyatt slowed to her pace, falling in behind. His heart rate slowed, returning to normal, his breathing regular and steady. Panic attack averted, he felt more normal, in control and aware of the time. As much as he liked following the pretty woman with the pink ass and the dark red, bobbing ponytail, he needed to get back and shower before he met the coordinator of the International Trade Convention.

Wyatt lengthened his stride and passed the woman, thankful that simply by jogging ahead of him, she'd brought him back to the present and out of a near clash with the crippling anxiety he refused to let get the better of him.

As he put distance between him and the woman in pink, he passed the shadow of a building. A movement out of the corner of his eye made him spin around. He jogged in a circle, his pulse ratcheting up, his body ready, instincts on high alert. The scuffle of feet made him circle again and stop. He crouched in a fighting stance and faced the threat, the memory of his abduction exploding in his mind, slamming him back to Somalia, back to the dry terrain of Africa and the twenty rebels who'd jumped him and Dane when they'd been leading a training exercise in the bush.

Instead of Somali militants garbed in camouflage and turbans, a small child darted out of his parents' reach and ran past Wyatt, headed toward the edge of the river.

His mother screamed, "Johnnie, stop!"

By the time Wyatt grasped that the child wasn't an al-Shabab fighter, the kid had nearly reached the edge.

Wyatt lunged for the boy and grabbed him by the scruff of the neck as the little guy tripped. Johnnie would have gone headfirst into the slow-moving, shallow water had Wyatt not snagged him at the last minute.

Instead of thanking Wyatt, the kid kicked, wiggled and squirmed until Wyatt was forced to set the boy on the ground. Then Johnnie planted the tip of his shoe in Wyatt's shin with razor-sharp precision.

Wyatt released him and bent to rub the sore spot.

Little Johnnie ran back to his mother, who wrapped her arms around the brat and cooed. Safe in his mother's arms, he glared at Wyatt.

Wyatt frowned, the ache in his shin nothing compared to the way his heart raced all over again.

The boy's mother gave Wyatt an apologetic wince and hugged her baby boy to her chest. "Thank you."

A small crowd had gathered, more because Wyatt, the parents and child blocked the sidewalk than because they were interested in a man who'd just rescued a child from a potential drowning.

His heartbeat racing, his palms clammy and his pulse pounding so loudly in his ears he couldn't hear anything else, Wyatt nodded, glancing around for an escape. Fuck! What was wrong with him? If he didn't get away quickly, he'd succumb this time. Where was the woman in the pink shorts when he needed her? Some of his panic attacks had been so intense he'd actually thought he was having a heart attack. He hadn't told his commander, or the psychologist assigned to his case, for fear of setting back his reassignment even further. He wanted to be back in the field where the action was. Where he was fighting a real enemy, not himself.

As it was, he'd been given this snowbird task of heading up the security for the International

Trade Convention. "Do this job, prove you're one hundred percent and we'll take it from there," Captain Ketchum had said. To Wyatt, it sounded like a load of bullshit with no promises.

Hell, any trained monkey could provide security for a bunch of businessmen. What did Ketchum think Wyatt could add to the professional security firm hired to man the exits and provide a visual deterrent to pickpockets and vagrants?

Wyatt had tried to see the assignment from his commander's point of view. He was a soldier barely recovered from a shitload of injuries caused by violent militants who set no value on life, limb and liberty. Sure, he'd been so close to death he almost prayed for it, but he was back as good as—

A twinge in his knee, made it buckle. Rather than fall in front of all those people, Wyatt swung around like he meant it and stepped out smartly.

And barreled into the woman he'd been following. Her head down, intent on moving, she'd been squeezing past him at that exact moment.

The female staggered sideways, her hands flailing in the air as she reached out to grab something to hold onto. When her fingers only met air, she toppled over the edge and fell into the river with a huge splash.

Another lady screamed and the crowd that had been standing on the sidewalk rushed to the edge of the river, pushing Wyatt forward to the point he almost went in with the woman.

A dark, wet head rose from the water like an avenging Titan, spewing curses. She pushed lank strands of hair from her face and glared up at him. "Are you just going to stand there and stare? Or are you going to get me out of this?"

Guilt and the gentleman in Wyatt urged him to hold out his hand to her. She grasped it firmly and held on as he pulled her out of the river and onto the sidewalk. She was so light, he yanked with more force than necessary and she fell against him, her tight little wet body pressing against his.

His arm rose to her waist automatically, holding her close until she was steady on her own feet.

The redhead stared up into his eyes, her own green ones wide, sparkling with anger, her pretty little mouth shaped in an O.

At this close range, Wyatt saw the freckles sprinkled across her nose. Instead of making her face appear flawed, they added to her beauty, making her more approachable, though not quite girl-next-door. She was entirely too sexy for that moniker. Especially all wet with her skin showing through the thin fabric of the lime green tank top.

Then she was pushing against him—all business and righteous anger.

A round of applause sounded behind him, though he didn't deserve it since he'd knocked her into the water in the first place. "My apologies, darlin'."

She fished the MP3 out of the strap around her arm and pressed the buttons on it, shaking her head. "Well, that one's toast."

"Sweetheart, I'll buy you a new one," Wyatt said, giving her his most charming smile. "Just give me your name and number so that I can find you to replace it."

"No thanks. I'm not your sweetheart and I don't have time to deal with it." She squeezed the water out of her hair and turned away, dropping the MP3 into a trashcan.

With her body shape imprinted in dank river water on his vest and PT shorts, he was reluctant to let her leave without finding out her name. "At least let me know your name."

She hesitated, opened her mouth to say something, then she shook her head as if thinking better of it. "Sorry, I've gotta go." She shrugged free of his grip and took off, disappearing into the throng of tourists on the River Walk.

Wyatt would have jogged after her, but the number of people on the sidewalk made it impossible for a big guy like him to ease his way through. Regret tugged at his gut. Although he hadn't made the best first impression on her, her bright green eyes and tight little body had given him the first twinge of lust he'd felt since he'd been in Somalia. Perhaps being on snowbird detail would help him get his mojo back. At the very least, he might find time, and a willing woman, to get laid. Okay, so a few days of R&R in a cushy assignment might not be too bad.

A flash of pretty green eyes haunted his every step as he wove his way through the thickening crowd to his hotel where he'd stashed his duffel bag. He wondered if in an entire city of people he'd manage to run into the red-haired jogger again. If so, maybe he could refrain from knocking her into the river next time and instead get her number.

Fiona Allen arrived at the door to her hotel room, dripping wet and in need of a shower to rinse off the not-so-sanitary San Antonio River water. She couldn't afford to come down with some disease this week. Not when dignitaries were already arriving for the International Trade Convention due to kick off in less than two days' time.

If she did come down with something, it would all be that big, hulking, decidedly sexy, beast of a man's fault. The one who'd knocked her into the river in the first place. When he'd pulled her out with one hand, he'd barely strained.

Her heart had raced when he'd slammed her up against his chest. She blamed it on the shock of being thrown into the river, but she suspected the solid wall of muscles she'd rested her hands against had more to do with it.

For a brief moment, she'd remained dumbstruck and utterly attracted to the clumsy stranger. Had it been any other circumstance and she hadn't been covered in river slime, she might have asked for his number. *Yeah, right.*

As the convention coordinator, she couldn't afford to date or be sick, or for anything to go wrong while thousands of businessmen and politicians attended the meetings. She'd been hired by the city to ensure this event went off without a hitch, and she wouldn't let a single disgruntled employee, terrorist or hulking bodybuilder knock her off her game. No sir. She had all the plans locked up tighter than Fort Knox and the hired staff marching to the beat of her military-style drum.

She wasn't the daughter of an Army colonel for nothing. She knew discipline; hard work and using your brain couldn't be replaced by help from sexy strangers with insincere apologies. If this convention was going to be a success, it would be so based on all of her hard work in the planning stages.

Once inside her room, she headed straight for the bathroom and twisted the knob on the shower, amazed at how much her breasts still tingled after being smashed against the broad chest of the clumsy oaf who'd knocked her into the river. She shook her head, attributing the tingling to the chill of the air conditioning unit.

In the bathroom, she stripped her damp gym shorts and tank top, dropping the soaked mess into a plastic bag. She'd hand it over to the hotel staff and ask them to launder them, otherwise she'd have nothing to work out in. Who was she kidding? She wouldn't need to work out once the convention began.

Fiona unclipped her bra and slid out of her panties, adding them to the bag of dirty clothes. Then she stepped beneath the shower's spray and attacked her body with shampoo and citrus-scented soap. Images of the muscle man on the River Walk resurfaced, teasing her body into a lather that had nothing to do with the bar of soap. Too bad her time wasn't her own. The man had certainly piqued her interest. Not that she'd find him again in a city of over a million people.

As she slid her soap-covered hand over her breast, she paused to tweak a nipple and moaned. It had been far too long since she'd been with a man. She'd have to do something about that soon. With her, a little sex went a long way. Perhaps she would test the batteries in her vibrator and make do with pleasuring herself. Although the device was cold and couldn't give her all she wanted, it was a lot less messy in so very many ways. Relationships required work. Building a business had taken all of her time.

Fiona trailed her hand down her belly to the tuft of curls over her mons and sighed. Maybe she'd find a man. After the convention when her life wasn't nearly as crazy. She rinsed, switched off the water and stepped out on the mat, her core pulsing, her clit throbbing, needy and unfulfilled.

With a lot of items still begging for her attention, she couldn't afford the luxury of standing beneath the hot spray of the massaging showerhead, masturbating. Towel in hand, she rubbed her skin briskly, her breasts tingling at the thought of the big guy on the River Walk.

By the time the convention was over, that man could be long gone. He probably was a businessman passing through, or one of the military men on temporary duty. Even if he lived in the city, what were the chances of running into him again? Slim to none. San Antonio was a big place with a lot of people.

Well, damn. She should have given him her name and number. A quick fling would get her over her lust cravings and back to her laser-sharp focus.

She dragged a brush through her long, curly hair, wishing she'd cut it all off. With the convention taking all of her spare time, she didn't have time to waste on taming her mane of cursed curls. Most of the time it was the bane of her existence, requiring almost an hour of steady work with the straightener to pull the curls out. Having left her clean clothes in the drawer in the bedroom, Fiona stood naked in front of the mirror as she blew her hair dry, coaxing it around a large round brush.

This convention was her shot at taking her business international. If she succeeded and pulled off the biggest event of her career without a hitch, other jobs would come her way on her own merit, not based on a recommendation from one of her stepfather's cronies.

When she'd graduated with her masters in Operations Management, she'd invested the money her mother had left her in her business, F.A. International Event Planner. Since then, she'd steadily built her client list from companies based in San Antonio. Starting out with weddings, parties and small gigs, she'd established a reputation for attention to detail and an ability to follow through. She'd worked her way in as a consultant for some of the larger firms in the area when they'd needed to plan a convention based in San Antonio.

Finally she'd gotten a lead on the International Trade Convention and had applied. Her stepfather put a bug in the ear of one of his buddies from his active Army days at the Pentagon and she'd landed the contract.

Now all she had to do was prove she was up to the task. If it fell apart, she'd lose her business, disgrace the U.S. government and shame her stepfather. The pressure to succeed had almost been overwhelming. To manage the workload, she'd taken out a big loan, more than doubled her staff, coordinated the use of the convention center, arranged for all the food, meeting rooms, audio-visual equipment, translators, and blocked out lodging and security for the guests.

As she dried her hair, she stared at the shadows beneath her eyes. Only a few more sleepless nights and the convention would be underway and over. She'd be playing the role of orchestra conductor, managing the staff to ensure everything was perfect. The most important aspect of the event was tight security. The Department of Homeland Security had notified her today that with all the foreign delegates scheduled to attend, the probability of a terrorist attack had risen to threat level orange.

A quick glance at her watch reminded her that she only had ten minutes to get ready before her meeting in the lounge with the man Homeland Security had insisted she add to her staff to oversee security. This last-minute addition made her nervous. She knew nothing about the man, his background or his capabilities. He could prove more of a hindrance than a help if he got in the way. All she knew was that he'd better be on time, and he'd better be good. With a hundred items roiling around in her head at any one moment, the last thing she needed was an international incident.

Fiona shut off the blow dryer, ran the brush through her hair and reached for the doorknob, reminding herself to look at the e-mail on her laptop from Homeland Security to get the name of the contact she'd be meeting shortly. Before she could turn the doorknob, it twisted in her hand and the door flew open.

A very naked man, with wild eyes and bared teeth shoved her up against the wall, pinned her wrists above her head and demanded, "Who the hell are you? And why are you in my room?"

Chapter Two

Wyatt had stopped in the hotel store for a can of shaving cream and a package of condoms. The shaving cream he had in his duffle, but it was getting low and the condoms... Well, after running into the pretty jogger in the pink shorts, he'd started thinking about sex again. He'd rather be prepared in case an opportunity presented itself.

A mother and a couple of kids got to the clerk first and proceeded to count out thirty-five pennies, five dimes and a quarter for a candy bar.

Wyatt glanced at the clock hanging on the wall behind the clerk. In fifteen minutes he was supposed to be in the lounge to meet with the convention planner. He could get a shower, shave and dress in less than ten, if the kids would hurry up and complete their purchase.

One of the children dropped more pennies on the floor. The two kids and their mother dropped to their haunches to collect the coins.

At that rate, he'd never get ready in time for his meeting.

Still, he couldn't be impatient with the children, their mother was trying to teach them it cost money for treats and how to pay for things they want. One of the pennies rolled toward his foot and he bent to pick it up.

The boy looked about the same age as Little Johnnie who'd kicked him in the shin, only this child smiled up at him instead of glaring. "Thank you, sir," he said. He had dark auburn hair and freckles on his nose.

Wyatt pictured the woman in the pink shorts as the mother of this child and immediately he glanced across at the child's mother who had a lighter shade of red hair and no freckles. Whew. He hadn't been lusting after someone's wife or mother—as far as he knew.

She helped the boy and the small girl hand over the change and grabbed the candy bar. "We'll split it after dinner. Come on, this gentleman has been waiting long enough."

"No hurry, ma'am," he assured her, even though he stood a strong chance of being late for his meeting with the event planner. F. Allen would just have to cool his heels. Wyatt was too sweaty from his jog to meet with anyone.

His purchases paid for, Wyatt retrieved his duffle bag from where he'd stashed it behind the concierge's desk and fished his key card, from an inside pocket. He'd checked in earlier, but his room hadn't been quite ready. Rather than stand around the lobby, he'd gone for a jog that served two purposes: blowing out the cobwebs and giving him a tactical lay of the land.

Key card in hand, he hurried to the elevator, a shower and a shave at the top of his priority list. He rode up to the floor he'd been assigned, slid his key card in the door lock and entered. As soon as the door closed behind him, he tossed his duffle bag next to the dresser, stripped out of his vest, gun and shorts and made a beeline for the bathroom, anticipating just enough time to make his meeting.

That was when he pushed the door open and ran chest-first into an intruder. His pulse leapt and he grabbed her hands, slamming her against the wall, his instincts on self-preservation. Surprise sharpened his voice as he said the first thing that came into his head. "Who the hell are you? And why are you in my room?"

After his gut reaction to slam the intruder against the wall, his mind had a full two-second delay before it engaged.

Wide green eyes stared up at him. Eyes he recognized from an earlier encounter beside the river. It was the redhead he hadn't stopped thinking about. And she looked pissed.

"Let go of me or I'll scream," she cried, her naked breasts pressing into his chest with every breath she took.

No longer on alert, he relaxed, but he didn't let go of her wrists. "Not until you tell me what you're doing in my room."

"*Your* room? This is *my* room and you're trespassing."

"I have a key and a receipt indicating this was the room assigned to me at the desk. Which means, darlin', you're in the wrong room."

"I have the same, and I don't appreciate being held captive without any clothes on.

Perhaps we can take this discussion down to the desk, *after* we've both had a chance to dress." Though her words were matter-of-fact and forceful, color had crept up her neck and bloomed in her cheeks.

Wyatt relented and released her wrists, stepping back, reluctantly. Too late, he realized his body had reacted to hers and his cock jutted out, hard and ready to take it from there.

Her gaze slipped down his length, pausing at that revealing appendage. "Holy shit." If possible, her cheeks grew even redder. She grabbed a towel and flung it at him. Then she ducked beneath his arm and dove for the bedroom dresser.

A chuckle rose up Wyatt's throat as he watched the smooth, rounded derriere dart past him. The pink shorts had nothing on the smooth pale, white flesh of her pretty bottom.

"A gentleman wouldn't stare," she said, her voice breathy as she jammed her feet into a pair of panties.

"I never claimed to be a gentleman." Wyatt wrapped the towel around him, the front tenting out. No matter how hard he tried to think his way out of the erection, seeing the redhead slide into her panties only made him harder.

"At the very least, you could turn around."

He shook his head. "Sorry, darlin'. I never turn my back on strangers. Especially if the stranger is trespassing in my room and has a sexy ass."

She huffed, grabbed a bra out of a drawer and turned her back to him, that very sexy bottom holding his interest more than he should admit, the thong panties doing nothing to cover the glorious orbs.

"I told you, this is *my* room. I reserved it months ago," she threw over her shoulder.

"Guess we'll have to let the desk clerk sort it all out."

When she turned back, dressed in a sexy black bra and matching lace panties, she planted her hands on her hips. "Why aren't you getting dressed?"

He nodded to the duffle bag on the floor beside the dresser. "Just waiting for you to move so that I can get to my clothes."

She stomped past him to the closet, pulled out a gray skirt suit and an orange sherbet blouse and faced him, holding the suit in front of her like a shield. "Do you mind?"

He shook his head. "Not at all." He remained leaning against the doorway to the bathroom. When she continued to stare at him pointedly, he straightened. "I take it you want me to let you by so that you can dress in the bathroom."

"That would be the gentlemanly—"

"—thing to do." His lips curled and he wanted to laugh out loud at her indignant expression. "How do I know you're not keeping a weapon in the bathroom?"

"Because I didn't carry a weapon into the bathroom. Go ahead. Check the bathroom. I might be hiding a fifty-caliber machine gun in there."

Wyatt shoved the door wider and glanced in, making a quick show of checking shelves, counters and behind the shower curtain. The only thing that caught his attention was the hot pink shorts lying in a half-open laundry bag on the floor. "All clear."

"Told you."

He crossed his arms over his chest, still not moving out of the doorframe. "I knew it. I'm just pushing your buttons, since you're trespassing in my room. Did you know your eyes flare when you're angry?"

The woman planted her fists on her gorgeous hips. "Then they should be flaring right now."

"I don't know why you'd bother to dress in the bathroom. You could dress out here and let me get my shower."

"I like having a lock on the door."

"What does it matter? I've already seen everything you have to offer."

"For the record, I'm not offering you anything. And I don't dress in front of jerks."

He nodded. "We've established I'm not a gentleman. Really, the repetition is getting boring."

She stomped a pretty little foot, her effort making little impression in the carpet, but she sure was cute with her long red hair hanging free around her shoulders.

Wyatt had the sudden urge to pull her into his arms and tangle his fingers in all the burnished copper strands. He moved aside, allowing her pass.

She walked past him into the bathroom, her head held high and slammed the door between them.

After barging in on her and holding her captive when she was naked, Wyatt figured he didn't have a snowball's chance in hell at getting her to go out with him. Not now. Still, he couldn't help trying. Those long, shapely legs would be nice wrapped around his waist, and he could just imagine how her pale white ass would fit in the palm of his hands as he pumped in and out of her. He glanced down at the tented towel and groaned. "It might help to know the name of the person who is trespassing in my room." He crossed the room to the duffle bag leaning against the far side of the dresser and removed a pair of jeans.

"Why would I tell you my name?" she asked through the door. "For all I know you're some pervert who gets off on breaking into a woman's room."

"I guess when you put it that way, you have a point." He grinned as he draped the jeans over his arm. "Only, since it's *my* room, *you* could be the pervert. Though that thought has some appeal." He pulled a chambray shirt from the bag, shaking out the wrinkles. The door to the bathroom opened as he draped the shirt over the jeans and waited for her to come out.

The redhead emerged from the bathroom, fully clothed in the soft gray suit and pale orange blouse, looking cool, calm and collected and every bit as sexy as she had in her bra and panties or stark naked.

What was it about this woman that had him so hot? Wyatt chalked it up to the months he'd been celibate. After he'd recovered from his injuries, he'd lacked any desire to find a woman and take her to bed. The shrink had claimed PTSD could lead to depression. Lack of desire was only one sign of depression.

Thankfully, the woman had reminded him he was definitely a healthy male capable of a raging hard-on. How to get her into bed would be the challenge.

She padded to the closet, stepped into light gray high-heeled pumps and finally faced him. Her eyes flared briefly when her gaze landed on his chest. Her hands clasped together and she swept her tongue around her bottom lip.

That tongue thing was almost Wyatt's undoing.

"How much longer until you're ready?" she asked, breaking into his mental picture of his tongue dueling with hers.

"Don't wait on me. I'm not getting dressed until I shower the sweat off my body." He doubted seriously he could walk at that point, with his cock tenting the towel around his middle.

"Not in *my* shower, you're not."

"Guess we'll be waiting here for a long time then."

She blew a stream of air out her nose. "Fine. Get your shower. And hurry it up. I'm not leaving you in my room. You might rob me."

He chuckled, loving the fire in her eyes and the color in her cheeks when she was angry. "I can't imagine what I'd do with panties and skirt suits."

She quirked her eyebrows upward. "Perverts do strange and disgusting things."

Oh, he could imagine all kinds of strange and disgusting things he'd like to do to her body. He crossed to the bathroom door. "I'm ready…" For more than she could imagine. And wouldn't she be appalled if she could read his mind? "…er, I'll be ready in less than five minutes." Closing the door behind him, he switched on the shower and stepped in even before the water warmed, hoping the cool shower would deflate his boner. He'd have a difficult time getting into his jeans as hard as he was.

The bathroom smelled like her, the shampoo some honeysuckle-scented perfection that reminded him of home in the Texas hill country and only made him crazier with need. With quick, efficient movements, he scrubbed the sweat off his skin and shampooed his short hair. When he ran a soapy hand down to his dick, he groaned. Damn he really needed to get laid. No woman should have that much of an effect on him. Rinsing in ice-cold water, he gave up and climbed out, toweling off with more speed than care.

As promised, less than five minutes later, he exited the bathroom, wearing uncomfortably tight jeans and sliding his arms into his chambray shirt. "Ready?"

Her brows furrowed. "Don't you think you should button up first?"

"I can do it on the way down in the elevator." Wyatt pulled his boots on and held the door open for her, waiting for her to pass. When she did, he inhaled the fragrant scent of honeysuckle in her hair.

She reached the elevator before him and jabbed the down button.

When the door slid open, she stepped in. Wyatt followed, slowly buttoning his shirt as the car slid toward the ground floor. By the way she glanced sideways at him, he figured he was getting to her. Either that, or the bright pink in her cheeks was the result of too much sun, a distinct possibility in Texas.

The elevator car stopped on the second floor and a group of teenage boys in matching baseball uniforms scrambled in, laughing and poking at each other.

The redhead eased to the back of the car, backing over Wyatt's boots. She wobbled and would have fallen if Wyatt hadn't slipped an arm around her middle to steady her. "Easy there, darlin'," he whispered against her ear.

She stiffened. "I'm not your darlin'," she said, her voice low, her comment meant for his ears only.

He liked that even though she'd started out stiff, by the time they reached the lobby level, she was leaning against him.

The boys piled out quickly, leaving Wyatt and the woman to exit at their own pace.

The redhead bolted, heading straight for the reception desk.

Wyatt hurried after her, a step behind, thinking *damn, she has a great ass* every step of the way.

Several people stood in line, many wearing business suits, some speaking Spanish, others speaking languages Wyatt wasn't as familiar with.

"Damn," the redhead muttered. "I don't have time to wait in line. I have a meeting in…" she glanced at her watch, "…three minutes."

Two of the people checking in gathered their key cards and documents and wheeled their suitcases off, opening up a clerk for the next two in line.

Wyatt glanced at his own watch. He'd be late for his meeting as well. "Next!" a female receptionist called out.

The redhead hurried toward her. "Excuse me, but there seems to be some confusion. This man claims he was assigned to the room I reserved over two months ago."

"Name, please?"

"Fiona Allen."

Finally a name to add to the beautiful face. Fiona. It suited her. She had that red Irish look to her, with the pale skin and freckles.

The clerk's fingers flew over the keyboard and she glanced up. "The system shows you in room three twenty-eight."

Fiona's head jerked up and she gave him a triumphant smile. "See? It's *my* room."

"Your name, sir?" the receptionist demanded.

"Wyatt Magnus."

Again the clerk's fingers skimmed across the keys. She frowned and hit a few more keys. Then she glanced to the side at the man wearing the manager nametag. "Scott," she called out.

Busy welcoming another guest, he ignored the clerk's entreaty.

"Scott!" she called out, louder this time.

Scott turned toward her, the smile he'd been sharing with a customer fading when he looked at the clerk's face. "What seems to be the problem?" He joined her at the monitor and added his frown to hers.

"It appears we've inadvertently double-booked the room," he said.

"What do I do?" the clerk asked.

"Assign Mr. Magnus another room," Fiona shot back as if it were the most obvious solution.

"But—" the clerk started to say.

"Here, let me." The manager brushed her aside and pounded the keys, glancing up only briefly. "We apologize for the inconvenience. With the International Trade Convention and the All-Star baseball tournament going on at the same time, we've been super busy and corporate loaded new software, just in case we didn't have enough to deal with. It'll only be a moment." He tapped the keys, frowned, tapped more keys and his frown deepened. "I'm sorry, but it seems that all the rooms are booked."

"What do you mean booked?"

"As in full," the manager said. "Let me call around and see if there are any other rooms available at the neighboring hotels." He lifted a telephone and called one hotel after another, each one reporting no vacancy. Finally, he glanced up. "I can get you into a motel on the outer loop."

Wyatt shook his head. "No can do. My business in San Antonio requires that I stay downtown, as close to the convention center as possible."

Fiona frowned. "Are you here for the International Trade Convention?"

He nodded. "Yes."

She smiled one of those, I-have-the-perfect-solution-that-doesn't-require-me-to-sacrifice smiles. "There will be park-and-ride bus service from strategic locations all across the city. I'm certain there will be a pick-up close to one of the outlying hotels."

"I need to be downtown." He captured Fiona's gaze. "You seem like a fair person, Fiona."

"I am. So?" Her eyes narrowed. "What does that have to do with this situation?"

"Well…" he started.

"I've had this reservation for months. I'm not giving up my room." She glanced at her watch and then shot a glance to the manager and clerk. "Look, I have a meeting to go to. When I get back, I expect a room…to myself…in *this* hotel."

"I don't know how we can make that happen," the manager said.

"I don't care how you make it happen. Your company made the error. Fix it." She spun on her gray high heels and marched away.

"Sir?" the clerk asked tentatively. "Would you consider going to another hotel?"

He chuckled. "For anyone else, maybe. But not for *her*. Let her stew." Giving the clerk and the manager an apologetic smile, he added, "Watch the cancellations. I'm sure something will free up. In the meantime, which way is the lounge?"

"Through the lobby and take a left at the elevator."

The snowbirding assignment was getting more interesting by the minute. Double-booked with the redhead in pink shorts had to be fate playing her tricky hand.

Wyatt wasn't sure how these cards would play out, but he was in for the hand and, if all went well, for the game.

Chapter Three

Fiona stomped all the way to the ladies' restroom, steaming. Mad and aroused, wrapped up in one tight knot of screaming nerves.

Holy hell!

Wyatt Magnus had to be the most aggravating man she'd met in a very long time. So what if his dark chocolate eyes smiling down on her made her knees go weak. And so what if having pressed her naked breasts to his equally naked chest had fired up a raging inferno at her very core. He was a beast. An ungentlemanly beast who would take advantage of a woman in a bad situation.

She punched the number for her assistant, Maddie Wells.

"Hey, boss," Maddie answered cheerfully. "I got the replacement quartet lined up for the meet-and-greet tomorrow night. They'll arrive an hour early and stay until midnight."

"Good. I—"

"I also got the florist to come down six hundred dollars on the table arrangements and they will deliver and set up, instead of having one of our vans and people do the job."

"Great. I—"

"Oh, and Carmelo DaVita, the delegate from Paraguay will be arriving late tonight. He prefers to have satin sheets on his bed. I called the hotel to make sure they arranged to have the bed made up in satin."

"Maddie!"

"I'm sorry. Did you have something you needed to say?"

"Yes." Fiona inhaled and let the breath out slowly, calming herself. "The hotel screwed up my reservation and double-booked me with an odious, pain-in-the-ass man." With broad shoulders, narrow hips and eyes she could totally fall into. And equipped? Oh yeah. Pulling her head out of the image, she said, "Stay on the phone with them until they fix it. I forgot to look and I'm already downstairs and late. Do you have the name of the man from Homeland Security?"

"No, do you need me to call?"

"No, no. I'll figure it out. Just stay on the hotel and get me another room."

"You're supposed to meet with the DHS rep now though."

"Yeah, I know. I'm on my way." Fiona muttered a curse. "How hard can it be to find some old government employee?"

"Deep breath," Maddie said. "It'll all work out. The fabulous Fiona Allen is on the job. She never lets a detail slide by her without tweaking the hell out of it."

Fiona's lips twisted as she pushed through the door to the ladies' room. "Let's hope I can tweak up a hotel room in the next hour or so. My feet are killing me."

"I'm on it like hair on a monkey's back." Maddie laughed and hung up.

In the bathroom, Fiona made quick work of the facilities, washed her hands and tried to make sense of her crazy curls. Well, hell. Short of chopping it off, nothing would ever bring her hair under control. It would have to do. Besides, it didn't matter for this meeting. The man Homeland Security had sent was bound to be an older government employee with poorly fitting clothing and worn shoes, and be completely clueless when it came to organizing a security staff of over fifty people.

The security firm she'd hired came highly recommended, fully vetted and bonded. They screened all their employees and trained them extensively. Fiona had full faith in them and thought the added layer of supervision redundant and frankly annoying.

Smoothing the nonexistent wrinkles out of her skirt, she left the bathroom and headed for the lounge. Her gaze darted to the reception desk. The man who'd wrecked her perfectly ordered day by first knocking her into the river and then stealing her room had disappeared.

Good.

Out of sight, out of mind.

Sadly, he was all over her mind and fully entrenched in her thoughts. Images of his naked body couldn't be wiped from her memory that easily, like they'd been permanently etched on her brain. The man had a great shape and he was by far the most well-endowed man she'd ever had the pleasure of viewing naked.

Her heart pounded and her palms moistened, along with other areas of her body she would prefer remained nameless. Yes, indeed, the man was hung like a—

As she stepped into the lounge, the man foremost in her thoughts appeared in front of her, seated at the bar, tipping a longneck beer back. He even made swallowing look sexy.

Aggravating man!

Determined to ignore him and get on with this untimely meeting with the rep from Homeland Security, she stood in the center of the room and made a 360-degree turn, searching for a likely candidate.

A couple sat at one of the tables, completely engrossed in each other. Four men sat at another, suit jackets hung over the backs of their seats, glasses of whiskey in front of them. Not one of them looked up from their conversation.

A man sat at a table nursing a martini, wearing slacks and a polo shirt with a logo for an aerospace company embroidered on the left breast. He stared into his drink, never once glancing up.

The only other man in the place stood beside the odious Wyatt Magnus. Or should she say swayed beside Wyatt. Five empty shot glasses were stacked in front of him and he waved to the bartender for another.

The bartender shook his head. "Sorry, mister, I believe you've had enough."

"Ah, don't be a party pooper. Jush one more." The man nearly fell off his seat, righted himself and raised one finger.

"Sorry." The bartender turned away and went back to stacking beer bottles in a cooler beneath the counter.

"Wass with the service 'round here?" the drunk exclaimed. "Can't a man get a drink?"

"Hey, buddy. Why don't I help you up to your room?" Wyatt suggested.

"I don't need help gettin' to my room. I'm perfeckly capable." He slid off his barstool and would have done a face plant on the floor if Wyatt hadn't caught him beneath his arms.

"That's right. You don't need any help." Wyatt grunted, straining under the man's weight.

One of the waiters rushed forward and looped the drunk's arm over his shoulder. Together, they half-walked, half-dragged the man toward the exit.

Much as she wanted to detest Wyatt Magnus, everywhere she turned, he was helping someone out. First the little boy who almost dove into the river, now this drunk. Most men would have let the guy hit the floor and left him for someone else to clean up.

Not Wyatt. He patiently hauled the guy out.

A bellboy met them at the door, insisting on taking over for Wyatt.

Relieved of his burden, Wyatt turned back toward the lounge and spotted her for the first time since the drunk fell all over him.

Fiona's heart stuttered and then raced, her belly tightening. She scrunched her damp hands into fists, digging her fingernails into her palms. Maybe that little bit of pain would keep her from drooling over the broad shoulders and dreamy eyes of the man who'd been a thorn in her side since she'd met him.

"That was nice of you," she admitted reluctantly.

"So now I'm nice?"

"I didn't say you were nice. The gesture was nice. I'm still mad at you for taking my room."

Wyatt motioned toward a barstool. "Can I buy you a drink?"

"No, thank you. I'm supposed to meet someone here." She glanced around and back down at her watch. "He was supposed to be here by now."

Wyatt's eyes narrowed briefly and then widened. His lips turned up at the corners in a very sexy smile. "I'm kinda slow on the uptake here, but let me guess—Fiona Allen. As in F. Allen of FA International Event Planners?" He shook his head. "I expected to meet a man, not…well, not you." He stuck his hand out. "Wyatt Magnus, sent here by my commander, on loan to the Department of Homeland Security to supervise the security for this convention."

Taken aback by Wyatt's revelation, she took his hand automatically as she scrambled for a functioning brain cell and a single coherent thought. "You?"

He chuckled, the sound warming her insides more than she ever cared to admit. "Me. Granted, it wasn't my idea. I'd much rather brave a deployment to Afghanistan than stand around checking for Boy Scout knives in businessmen's pockets."

"This will never do." Fiona swallowed hard. "I can't work with you."

Wyatt almost laughed out loud at the way the blush rushed up Fiona's neck and she pressed her hands to her cheeks. The woman was far too uptight and stirring the sand in her sandbox suited Wyatt perfectly.

"Sorry, but I'm on orders."

"What do you mean *on orders?*" She shook her head. "I'm telling you, I don't need you here. I have a perfectly good security firm with fifty guards lined up to handle the security of the convention center and this hotel. They'll have metal detectors in place and will perform whatever pat downs need to be done."

"That's all well and good for checking for weapons on people entering. What about bombs and improvised explosive devices?"

"We aren't allowing vehicles to park close the convention center. It will be cordoned off to keep that from happening." She crossed her arms. "So you see, you're services are not needed."

"Did you consider that not all bombs are going to arrive in a truck? Plastic explosives are hard to detect with metal detectors. Do you have bomb-sniffing dogs lined up to sweep the convention center before the party begins?"

Her brow furrowed. "Not that I know of. I'll put a call into the security firm."

"No, I'll call them. From now until the convention is over and the foreign dignitaries have departed, the security firm will be reporting directly to me."

"No way. I'm not having some stranger I know nothing about circumvent all the planning I've put into this event." Fiona pulled out her cell phone and scrolled through her contact list and then hit a number. As she raised the phone to her ear, her eyes narrowed. "As soon as I clear this up, you will no longer need a room and you can crawl back under whatever rock you came out of."

Wyatt shoved his hands into his jeans pockets and rocked back on his heels. He knew what the answer would be before Fiona said hello.

His commander had specifically stated that he was directed to provide one of his best men to head up the security. His commander's orders came straight from the Pentagon. Probably from the same place Fiona was now calling.

Fiona turned, walked a few steps away and stood with her back to him, her voice low and determined. "You have to be kidding. This was not in my contract," she was saying.

A grin slipped across Wyatt's lips.

"It is? Well, it must have been in the fine print, because I would not have agreed to these conditions." She listened for a moment, her body stiff, her hand squeezing the phone so tightly her knuckles turned white. "How many of those do you get a day?" She nodded. "You do? And it came in this morning?" Fiona pushed her long red hair back from her forehead. "Fine. He can stay. But I won't have him making a disaster of it. He will report to me every step of the way or you can find someone else to finish this event." She clicked the end button. Her chest expanded as she sucked in a deep breath and then let it out before she turned.

"Was I right?" Wyatt queried.

"You know damn well you were." She poked a finger at his chest. "If the FBI hadn't received a report of a threat that came across their desk this morning specifically targeting the convention, I'd send you packing. Unfortunately, the Pentagon trusts that you're the man for the job." She snorted. "Not that I fathom why. But you report to me. Don't make a single change without consulting with me first."

He tried to school the smile from his face as he raised his index finger. "I'd like to suggest change number one."

Fiona rolled her eyes and clamped her jaw tight. "Go on."

"I'd like to bring in bomb-sniffing dogs to sweep the convention center tomorrow, first thing, before any conventioneers arrive."

"And how do you propose to bring on enough dogs to perform this sweep on such short notice? This convention took months of planning."

Wyatt's grin widened. "I have a buddy who runs a dog training business here in San Antonio. He has search and rescue, protection, drug control and bomb-sniffing dogs available in his kennel." At the skeptical frown on her forehead. "He owes me a favor."

He'd saved Joseph Goodman from a burning vehicle when their convoy had come under attack by Taliban in Afghanistan. His vehicle had taken a direct hit and crashed into a wall. Joseph suffered compound fractures in both legs and burns on his arms. If Wyatt hadn't been there to pull him out, he'd have died in the fire. As it was, Joe's legs would never be the same and he walked with a limp. He'd spent weeks at SAMC's burn center for the burns on his hands and arms. The military had medically retired him and he had nothing to look forward to. No job, no home, no purpose in life.

Deep in depression, he had no motivation to recover. Once the external wounds healed, he'd gone to a rehab facility. He'd been there when a local organization that specialized in training dogs for service had come through. The handler brought with her a golden retriever, trained to provide comfort to soldiers with PTSD. One touch and Joe had known what he wanted to do.

It still choked up Wyatt to think about Joe's recovery. He'd been in the depths of depression when he'd been laid up in the hospital. More than anything, he'd wanted to get back to the fight, to defend his brothers in arms. Yet, here he was, safe on American soil, away from the turbulence of war, the uncertainty of each day. Kind of like Wyatt. Only Joe had found a purpose.

"Fine." Fiona's word cut through his memories like a knife, bisecting the real world from the past. "Get the dogs. I'll figure out how to pay for them. But I'm warning you, I don't have much wiggle-room. The catering and convention center costs took up most of my funds."

"I'm sure he'll give me the best deal he can."

"Good, and while you're at it, see if he can put you up at night. I need that room more than you do."

Wyatt shook his head. "Sorry. As the man in charge of the security of this convention, I need to be as close to the convention center as possible."

"Fine. My assistant is working on it. She'll come up with a room for you somewhere close by."

"And where are the majority of the high-powered delegates staying?"

Her brows puckered. "Here."

"Aren't you having a social event here?"

She nodded.

"Exactly. Security is not all about the convention center."

"I can't be expected to provide security for every one of the participants."

"No, but if the most politically inclined are staying at this hotel, I need to be here to ensure everything that can be reasonably done is being done."

She chewed on her bottom lip, the frown deepening.

Wyatt could almost see the gears turning in her brain.

"Let's talk to the front desk again. Surely by now, they'll have a cancellation."

They exited the lounge and returned to the reception desk where a crowd had gathered. Ten men in business suits, an equal number of police officers and the hotel manager stood in front of the desk. One police officer stood with a clipboard, questioning one of the men in a business suit. He spoke Spanish and wrote as the man in the suit fired words back at him.

Fiona pushed through the crowd to the manager, Wyatt on her heels.

"What's going on?" she asked.

"Oh dear, Ms. Allen." He nodded toward the man speaking Spanish. "Jesus Rodriguez, the political delegate from Columbia, was on the way from the airport to the hotel when someone shot as his limousine."

"What?" Fiona exclaimed. "Who? Where?"

"That's why the police are here. They're taking his statement."

Wyatt suspected that the shot taken at the limousine was some dumbass taking a pot shot at the pretty, expensive car. But was it more than that? Was this the reason he'd been called in to head up the security? The piece of cake job might be more interesting than he first thought.

The manager gave Fiona an apologetic look. "By the way, I had a cancellation."

Fiona's face brightened. "That's great."

Wyatt didn't think it was. In fact, he was somewhat disappointed at the news.

"Ms. Allen, Mr. Rodriguez is demanding a room for the additional bodyguard he wants on the premises to protect him while he's here. What do you want me to do?"

Wyatt choked back a chuckle. The redhead couldn't win. "Give him the room," he whispered near her ear.

"What, and let you have our room?" She chewed her lip some more. "It's even more important for me to be in the same hotel. I need to be where the high-profile delegates are staying."

"Same here," Wyatt said. "Even more so." He crossed his arms. "How about this...we share the room—" He raised his hand when she started to open her mouth. "Hear me out, please."

"Fine. Talk. But make it quick. The manager needs to find you a room."

"I'll bet they have a rollaway cot we can put in the room. I can sleep on the cot—I've slept on worse—you can have the bed and we can take turns in the shower."

"No."

"At least until the manager has another cancellation."

"I'm not sleeping in the same room as you. I don't even know you. You could be a pervert, or worse."

Wyatt gave her his most convincing smile. "Or I could be nice guy forced to share a room with a very inflexible event planner. I can be trusted. If you don't believe me, check my references." He handed her his phone. "Call my boss. Better yet—" he took back his phone, "—call your contact with the government. They can get a background check on me faster, and they're not biased."

She glared at him. "I need the room to myself. How am I supposed to work with someone else in there?"

"The room is to sleep in. And I'll be out checking on security staff at the convention center during the day and into the evening hours."

The manager had been watching their exchange, his gaze shifting from Fiona to Wyatt and back with each verbal lob. Finally, he glanced at his watch. "Ms. Allen, I need an answer. The hotel is full and my people are working with a system that has proven less than reliable. I need to help them out."

Fiona nodded. "Fine. You can give the bodyguard the open room. Mr. Magnus and I will share our room. *If* you can get us a rollaway bed. Now all I need is a gun to tuck under my pillow in case he tries anything funny."

The manager's eyes widened. "Ms. Allen, talking about guns might not be prudent at this time." He nodded toward the cops.

Fiona flipped her hair back over her shoulder. "Fine." Then she turned to Wyatt and whispered for his ears only, "I *will* be checking on your references and I have my concealed carry license, so I will be packing should you think you can take advantage of me when we're alone."

Wyatt wanted to laugh out loud and would have if he didn't think she was serious. Fiona Allen carrying a gun scared him almost as much as the radical and dangerous Somali militants. But he wouldn't let her know that. He'd just have to show her how trustworthy he could be.

Following her up to their shared room, he began to wonder if he could keep his hands to himself. The sway of her hips and the ramrod straight back on her petite frame practically begged to be loosened. And he knew just how to massage the stiffness out her. *If* she'd let him close enough, and *if* she didn't shoot him first.

Chapter Four

Fiona swiped her card and entered the room first, every nerve cell in her body completely aware of the man behind her. What had she been thinking? She couldn't share a room with a perfect stranger.

And based on her earlier observations of his naked body, he was perfect in every physical way possible. All the more reason why she couldn't sleep in the same room with him.

Hell, sleep would be the furthest thing from her mind. As another thought occurred to her, her pulse leapt and heat rose up her throat into her cheeks. Did he sleep naked? *Holy hell.*

She made an abrupt about face. "I'm sorry. This isn't going to work."

"So you'll be leaving?" he asked.

"No, *you* will."

He shook his head. "I've done my share of sleeping on the hard ground. I'm in a hotel, not a campground. If you want to leave and let me have the room, fine."

A knock on the door made Fiona jump.

Wyatt opened it to a bellboy with the rollaway.

Just when she didn't think it could be worse, the bellboy had to be prompt.

"Where do you want it?" he asked.

Wyatt pointed to a space near the desk and an easy chair. "Right there for now."

The bellboy parked the bed where indicated and left the room before Fiona spoke again.

"You're not staying," she said.

"Relax. You'll barely know I'm here."

Like hell. He was all she could focus on. His broad shoulders practically filled the room, making it feel smaller with each breath she inhaled. "Look, I'm not happy about this situation. I like my space and, frankly, you're invading it."

"I'm here for the job, sweetheart, not you. Besides…" he cupped her cheek with his big, callused hand, "…you're not my type."

The warmth of his hand on her face made her want to lean into his palm, until his words hit her like a splash of chilled water. She straightened away from that dratted hand. "What do you mean?"

"About the job or the type?" He grinned, raising her ire another notch.

"Not your type? Just what *is* your type?"

His grin broadened, those full, kissable lips doing funny things to her insides. "Well, you got part of it right earlier. The naked part. But I also like my women willing." He winked, grabbed his duffle bag and dropped it on the rollaway. "Now, if you'll excuse me, I need to pay a visit to my buddy with the dogs."

"And I have to head over to my office for an hour or two." She glanced around the room again before shooting a narrow-eyed glare at him. "Don't touch my things."

He gave her mock salute. "Yes, ma'am."

"And don't call me ma'am. I'm not that old."

"Yes, ma'am. I mean...Fiona." He cupped her cheek again and leaned in until his lips hovered over hers. "A beautiful name for a beautiful woman."

Knowing it was all wrong but unable to stop herself, she leaned closer until their lips connected. A jolt of electricity shot through her, instantly heating places she'd thought cold for a long time.

Wyatt's hand slipped behind her neck and he applied pressure, his mouth taking hers in a deep, satisfying kiss.

When his tongue swept across hers, she opened eagerly, her tongue greeting his hungrily. Her brain disengaged and her body took over. Fiona slid her hands up his chest. When she should have been shoving him away, she linked her fingers behind his neck and pressed her breasts to his chest. She slid her leg up the back of his, her pussy pressing against the thick muscle of his thigh, an ache building deep in her core.

Wyatt's hands slipped beneath her shirt and up her ribs, his thumbs brushing against her breasts. In that moment, she wished she was as naked as she'd been at their earlier meeting. The way he touched her made the bones in her legs dissolve. Why did he have to be so damned attractive with his muscular body and high-and-tight haircut? Couldn't the government find a white-haired old man to oversee the security of this shindig? She could handle that.

When he broke off the kiss, he leaned his forehead against hers and chuckled. "I didn't see that coming."

Knowing she was as much at fault for initiating that kiss as he was, she stepped away, scrubbing her hands down the front of her skirt. If he hadn't backed off first, where would that kiss have led? Butterfly wings beat against the insides of her belly and her glance darted to the bed, and a sharp pull of longing swelled inside. This was wrong on so many levels. She wasn't sure how sharing a room with Wyatt would turn out, but it couldn't end up good.

Or it could end up way too good... Her insides tightened and a thrill of anticipation raced through her body. How long had it been since she'd had sex?

No, this was not how she envisioned this event starting.

Eager to get to the office and out of the overwhelming presence of Wyatt Magnus, she moved toward the door. "Gotta go."

"Me too."

She held up her hand. "For the sake of sanity, give me a head start. I need some time to think."

"As you wish, darlin'," he said with a serious poker face. Then he ruined it with a sexy grin. "Hopefully, you'll spend some time thinking of me."

"Don't flatter yourself," she shot back at him. Then she made a dash for the elevator before he could see the blush rising in her cheeks, or notice how she couldn't keep her gaze off him. Fiona knew what lay beneath the clothing and the thought of him lying in a bed near hers, possibly naked... Well, it didn't bear imagining. Nothing was going to happen. She had far more serious things to worry about than if he would make a pass at her. Or worse...that he wouldn't make a pass.

As she stepped into the elevator, she shot a glance down the hallway. Wyatt stood at the doorway of their room, a smile still fixed to his face that broadened when her gaze met his.

Damn. He'd caught her staring.

A warm, rich chuckle filled the hallway, like he knew the secret of what was to come later that night.

Fiona dove into the elevator, her cheeks burning, a place farther south flaming to life.

Holy hell. How was she going to get through the next few days with Wyatt Magnus's larger than life body to bump into everywhere she turned?

Wyatt was still grinning as he closed the door behind him and made certain it was securely locked and then adjusted his jeans. His groin was far too tight, but it had been worth the kiss to see the event planner's reaction. He'd made the calm, cool and efficient Fiona Allen run like a frightened rabbit. Oh yeah, he had definitely made an impression on her. Good. Because she'd made an equal one on him and he needed to shake it off so he could see to the security of the convention.

Sleeping in the same room with the fiery redhead would be a challenge. If he planned on sleeping. The real challenge would be to get her to agree to share her bed with him. A couple nights with Fiona ought to get him back on track sexually.

Rather than take the elevator, he headed for the stairwell, jogging down the steps until he reached the garage level. His Jeep was where he'd left it and he climbed in, pulling out his cell phone. Before he put the shift in gear, he dialed Joe.

"Dogs are Heroes, Joe speaking."

"Joe, Wyatt Magnus here."

"Wyatt, you old bulldog, what are you doing in town?"

A flash of guilt washed over Wyatt. He'd been in town for weeks and this was his first call to his friend. "It's a long story, but I need your help with bomb-sniffing dogs at the downtown convention center."

"What the hell? Did you quit the Army?"

"No, no. I'm on loan to Homeland Security to provide oversight for the security of the International Trade Convention."

"I thought you were in Ethiopia or Somalia or some other godforsaken country."

"I was. It's part of that long story I'll fill you in on later." He sighed. "In the meantime the convention starts tomorrow night and I want to make sure the threats we've been getting don't happen."

"Wow, who'd you piss off to get that assignment?"

Wyatt chuckled. "It's temporary. So what do you say? Do you have the resources?"

"Sure. I'm on the tail end of training fifteen dogs to be used at airports with the TSA. I can have them loaded and delivered by morning."

"Good. Can you meet me in an hour at the convention center to discuss the plan with the security firm the planner hired?"

"Which security firm?"

"Lone Star Security."

"They come highly recommended," Joe confirmed. "I haven't heard anything bad about their work. But you never know when you'll get a bad egg waiting to explode."

"Right. That's where you and your canines come into it."

"Keeping everyone on the up and up."

"We've already had one incident with the Columbian delegate. Shots were fired at his limousine."

"I heard about that on the police scanner."

"All the more reason for you to meet me at the convention center."

"I'll be there." Joe told Wyatt what entrance he'd be at and rang off.

Wyatt dug out the card Fiona had given him for the person in charge of the convention center security team for the next few days. Preston Jones.

He keyed the numbers and waited for the man to pick up on the other end. While he waited, he scanned the parking lot of the hotel. If they wanted to keep the delegates safe, he needed to check with hotel security. It wouldn't hurt to add a few guards to the mix. And he'd check out the cameras to ensure all were functioning and monitored.

Someone exited the building and walked quickly to a shiny black Mustang convertible. By the twitch of her skirt and the long, flowing red curls hanging down her back, there was no mistaking Fiona Allen.

Wyatt's pulse quickened and he couldn't tear his gaze away from her as she slid into the sports car and drove past him.

"Lone Star Security, Preston Jones speaking."

The male voice in his ear brought Wyatt back to the task at hand and he introduced himself.

"I've been expecting your call," Preston said. "I cleared my afternoon to meet with you and show you what we've done to get ready."

"I'm headed to the convention center now."

"I can meet you there in fifteen minutes."

"Good." Wyatt hung up and shifted his Jeep into drive, pulling out of the parking garage into the glare and heat of the south Texas sunshine.

Now that he had his meetings set up, he could get to work. The sooner this convention was over, the sooner he could get back to his real job with the Special Operations command.

When the convention was over, he'd leave San Antonio. A quick fling with the pretty little redhead wouldn't hurt in the meantime. It would get his motor revved and his spirits up. Yeah, a quick affair with the redhead might be just what the shrink ordered.

Maddie met Fiona at the door to her office, electronic tablet in hand. "I called the caterer, they had a hiccup in the menu and won't be serving cherry cheese cake. Instead it'll be caramel chocolate cheesecake. All's good though because the menu only states cheesecake."

Fiona strode through the outer office to her inner sanctum with Maddie on her heels.

"The string quartet I got to replace the original for tomorrow's welcome reception is down to a trio. One member is out sick. They assure me the music will be just as good. I called around to see if I could get someone else, but everyone is booked or out of town."

"Whatever." Fiona plunked her purse on her desk and stared at the order that was her desk, drinking in the fact that everything had a place. Order made her feel in control.

Perhaps that was why she was so upset by the day's events. Being around Wyatt made her feel completely out of control and chaotic. She planned the hell out of events with contingency plans in place in case the originals didn't work out. She didn't see a hotel reservation as risky or she would have booked two rooms on the off chance someone was double-booked in one.

The room grew so quiet, Fiona turned to her assistant.

Maddie stood with her hand on her hip.

"What?" Fiona said.

"Whatever?" Maddie stared at her as if she'd grown antennae. *"Whatever* from a boss who manages everything down to the most minute detail?"

Fiona shoved a hand through her hair, her fingers getting tangled. "Oh Maddie, this day has been insane."

"Yeah, and since when do you wear your hair down during the day?" Maddie shook her head. "What's got you rattled, oh gracious control freak?"

An image of Wyatt standing naked in her hotel room flashed in her mind. Fiona turned toward the window, feeling the heat rush up into her cheeks. "Did you have any more luck getting me a room than I did?"

"No. Their system is fouled up and they've double-booked several foreigners. They want to place them first since you live in the city."

"That's the right thing to do. Still…" She inhaled and let out a long breath.

"Can't you get the man to give up the room you two are double-booked in?" Maddie joined Fiona by the window.

"He needs to be there as much as I do."

"Is he one of the foreign delegates?"

"No, he's the man Homeland Security sent to oversee security of the convention. There are no other rooms in the downtown area."

"What are you going to do?"

"We've agreed to share the room." When Fiona said the words, she knew how crazy the idea sounded.

"You're sharing a room with a strange man?" Maddie's brows furrowed. "Want me to run a background check on him? He could be a serial killer or rapist."

Fiona's lips tipped upward on the edges. "He's military and on loan with Homeland Security. I've already run it up the chain of command. I'm stuck with him on the project."

"But you're not stuck sleeping in the same hotel room." Maddie lifted the phone and started dialing.

"Who are you calling?"

"The hotel. This will never do." Maddie held the phone to her ear.

Fiona took it from her. "Don't bother. I've already talked until I'm blue in the face. The hotel is booked. It's sleep in the streets or share a room with Wyatt."

"Wyatt?" Maddie set the phone back on the desk. "You two are already on a first name basis?"

Fiona's cheeks warmed all over again. Hell, they'd seen each other completely naked. They ought to be on a first name basis. "Yes. He'll be reporting directly to me about the security. He's already come up with a good idea." Why she hadn't thought of running bomb-sniffing dogs through the convention center was a mistake that could have cost her.

"The point is he's got to be nearby. We've already had an incident." Fiona explained about the shooting.

"Well, crap. Things couldn't go smoothly, could they?"

"There's a lot of unrest between some of the countries attending. I had hoped everyone would get along while they were here. And then the shooting had to happen. We don't know who's responsible yet. The police are looking into it." Fiona glanced at Maddie, her lips twisting in a wry grin. "In the meantime, I'm sharing a room with the head of security."

Maddie's eyes narrowed. "Want me to come stay with you? I'm sure I can convince my boyfriend that sharing a room with my boss and a strange man is perfectly acceptable."

"Sounds crazy, doesn't it?" Fiona's lips pressed together. "As much as he's annoying, I trust him not to do anything stupid." Perhaps that was why she'd agreed to share the room. That and he made her blood burn through her veins and the thought of catching him naked again... Damn. She had to get her mind out of the gutter. The man was there on a mission and so was she. "I'll be all right."

"You have that pepper spray I gave you last Christmas?"

Fiona nodded. "On my keychain."

"Leave it on the nightstand and use it if he gets too friendly." Maddie crossed her arms. "I don't like it."

"I promise I'll be okay."

"I have a mind to check in on you tonight. I could have a little chat with the squatter and let him know in no uncertain terms that he's to keep his hands to himself."

Fiona laughed. "Thank you, Mother, but that won't be necessary." A naughty thought insinuated itself into her head. What if he didn't keep his hands to himself? Maybe she wanted him to touch her. After the kiss they'd shared in the room, she was sure there was enough attraction to lead to more. Did she want it?

Maddie's gaze narrowed even more. "Just how old is this DHS guy? Is he a fatherly type?"

The heat burned in Fiona's cheeks again and she didn't turn away fast enough to avoid Maddie's pointed stare.

Her eyes widened. "He's not, is he?" Maddie grabbed Fiona's hands and forced her to face her. "Crap, Fiona, tell me all about him. Is he tall, is he handsome, is he nice?" A grin spread across her face. "You do realize you haven't had a boyfriend in at least a year. It's about time you got laid."

Fiona tried to shake free of Maddie's grip. "Oh please. It's not a crime to be without a boyfriend. I simply haven't had time."

"Ha! You *do* plan on getting laid." Maddie whooped. "You go, girl. Take charge of your sex life and rev it up."

"Really, Maddie. I have no plans to get laid."

"You can't plan everything, sweetie. Some things have to be spontaneous. The important thing is...does he make you hot? Is there any fire between the two of you? Has he kissed you?"

The more Maddie pushed for information, the hotter Fiona's cheeks burned.

"He has!" Maddie hugged Fiona. "I'm so happy for you. A kiss is just the beginning. Tonight you need to meet him in the bar in that little black dress that shows off your figure so well."

"I'm not dating the man. I'm just sharing a room with him. The kiss could very well have been a mistake on his part."

"But not on yours?" Maddie shivered. "Makes me wish I could be a fly on the wall tonight in your hotel room."

"Maddie! I never knew there was a naughty voyeur in you."

Maddie gave her a wicked smile. "Only because you never asked. My boyfriend and I belong to a BDSM club and they have a voyeur viewing room."

Fiona poked her fingers into her ears. "I don't want to hear this."

"Oh come on, Fiona. You're not that old. BDSM can be a lot of fun. You should bring Wyatt. I'm sure I can get you in for a trial run."

"No, no, no. Get this straight. Wyatt and I are sharing a room. Not a bed, not sex, not BDSM. He's not my boyfriend and he's not my lover. The end."

Maddie pouted. "Spoilsport. You really need to loosen up. Life is going to pass you by if you're not careful."

"I have a convention to run. I suggest we get back to what's important."

"Yes, ma'am." Maddie left Fiona in her office, and giggled all the way back to her desk. "Methinks the boss has met her match," she muttered loud enough Fiona could hear.

"He's not my match!" Fiona slammed the door between them.

Alone in her office, she could no longer ignore the fantasies that had plagued her all the way across town. Her body was on fire, her core hot and wet.

No stranger to pleasuring herself, she clicked the lock on the door and went to her desk where she kept her little secret. A shiny silver bullet vibrator that fit in the palm of her hand.

Maybe if she got herself off, she wouldn't be so aroused by Wyatt when she met up with him later.

She swept the papers on her desk to the side, pulled her skirt up to her waist and sat on the edge of the polished mahogany, thankful she'd worn thong panties. The cool wood surface did little to chill the rise of desire thrumming through her veins.

Fiona switched on the vibrator and let it shake in her palm for a few seconds, warming the cool metal. This was crazy. Maddie had given her the vibrator for her birthday, along with a sexy nightie and permission to seduce a man. She'd tucked the tiny tool away, preferring to use the larger one she kept in her nightstand at home. In private. What professional businesswoman fired up her vibrator in the office?

The vibrator had remained in her drawer for the past six months, unused, untested, tucked behind her pain medication for the occasional headache. What kind of medication was a vibrator?

She hoped it was the right kind to get her over her lusty feelings toward the naked security supervisor.

Spreading her legs wide, she imagined Wyatt stepping between them and rubbing his big cock against her clit. She parted her folds and pressed the pulsing device against the highly sensitive strip of flesh packed with what felt like thousands of little nerve endings, begging to be fired up.

At the first touch, her breath caught in her throat. Dipping it into her pussy, she coated the magic bullet in her juices and slid it back over her clit, the vibrations bringing her senses to attention, firing off synapses throughout her body.

She pictured herself naked, Wyatt dropping to his knees, draping her legs over his broad shoulders. He'd flick his tongue over that nubbin, again and again.

Fiona tapped the vibrator over her clit, pretending it was Wyatt's tongue. Her breathing grew more ragged, her body tightening, her core so hot she might spontaneously combust on her desk.

When she was close to the edge of orgasm, she slipped the bullet into her pussy and clenched around it, while finger flicking her clit.

"Oh my," she moaned, her finger working faster, trying to match the pulsing beat of the vibrator. "Oh yeah. There. Right there." Fiona threw back her head, her back arching, her finger doing double-time as the vibrator shook inside her.

Tingles began at her center and shot outward to the very tips of her fingers and toes. She held her breath as tremors of lust rippled across her body. For a long moment, she cupped her sex, the vibrator charging on until the last of the orgasm faded.

A knock on the door made her jerk the vibrator out. "Y-yes?" she said, her voice hoarse. Clearing her throat she aimed for her usual clear tone. "What is it?"

"I thought I heard you call out," Maddie said. "Is everything all right in there?" The doorknob wiggled. "Why is this door locked?"

"I was just resting my eyes. I'll be out in a moment." Fiona hopped off the desk and nearly fell flat on her face when her heel caught the carpet and sent her flying forward. Once she'd righted herself, she wrapped the vibrator in a tissue and stuffed it into her purse and slung the strap over her shoulder. On her way to the door, she tugged her skirt into place and patted her hair, pleased she'd been able to provide her own orgasm without the help of a man.

Well, almost. Fantasizing about a certain man didn't count. It could be any man, not the one she'd be sleeping with that night.

When she stepped through the door, she gave Maddie a cool smile. "I'm on my way to the convention center and I won't be back to the office today. Call me if you need me."

"One thing before you go, boss." Maddie's lips quirked upward on one side.

"I'm not going to have sex with Wyatt Magnus, so save your breath." Fiona was proud of herself remaining firm on that subject and for having taken care of her own needs.

"I wasn't going to say anything about getting laid by the sexy security guy." Maddie made an attempt to wipe the smile off her face, failing miserably. "I just thought you might want to know that your skirt is tucked into the back of your thong panties and your ass is showing."

"Oh, good grief." Her face flaming, Fiona yanked the back of her skirt down over her bottom. "Am I covered?"

"Yes, ma'am." Grinning broadly now, Maddie waved. "That silver bullet does the trick, doesn't it?"

She never could pull one over on Maddie. "Yes, it does. Let's hope it holds me through the night." Fiona paused at the exit. "And thank you for the gift."

"Just glad you're getting some use out of it. Although the real thing is so much better."

"I'll keep that in mind for the future. *After* the convention."

Her resolve strengthened by her release, she headed for the convention center, charged with the wicked thrill of anticipation as unavoidable as breathing.

Chapter Five

Wyatt met Joe Goodman on the front steps of the convention center.

His friend had brought with him a black and tan German Shepherd on a thick leather lead. When Joe stopped, the animal stopped and sat automatically, his tail sweeping the floor in a steady motion.

"So what gives, Magnus?" Joe stuck out his hand.

Wyatt gripped it and pulled the former linebacker and Special Ops soldier into a bear hug.

"Good to see you, man. How's the rehab going?"

Joe nodded. "Okay. The dogs helped me come through better than anything the Army could provide, although the staff at SAMC was great."

"Yeah, I know."

"Tell me." Joe leveled a stare at Wyatt. "I did some checkin'. Seems you did some time at SAMC yourself recently."

Wyatt nodded. "Not as bad as what you went through. A few holes, broken bones and messed up head. I'm headed back after TDY with the International Trade Convention."

"Good for you." Joe stared at the convention center. "Not a day goes by that I don't wish I could go back."

"Why?" Wyatt waved toward the dog at his feet. "You've got everything any man could ask for. Unconditional love, a job you can get passionate about and you're helping other vets." Wyatt bent to scratch the dog's ears. "You've got it all here. Seriously." Wyatt straightened. "You look better than the last time I saw you."

Joe snorted. "Last time you saw me, I was bleeding like a stuck pig. I wouldn't have made it had you not gotten me out of the hot zone so quickly. Thanks again."

Wyatt shrugged. "You'd have done the same for me."

"Damn right. You still owed me money for that poker game you lost to me."

"That's right. I forgot all about that. What was it, twenty bucks?" Wyatt reached into his back pocket.

With a shake of his head, Joe put his hand up. "I don't want your money."

"I pay my debts."

"It's me who can't repay you," Joe said. "But if it'll make you feel better, buy the animal shelter a bag of dog food and donate it in my name."

"I'll do that. And you owe me nothing." Wyatt nodded toward the convention center. "I'm supposed to meet the man in charge of additional security staff inside. What say we get to work?"

"I'm in." Joe glanced down at his dog. "Bacchus needs some exercise too." Together, they entered the building in search of Arthur Salazar, the dedicated security staff supervisor, and Preston Jones, the man in charge of the additional security staff hired by Fiona to help ensure the safety of the convention goers.

He found both of them in the equipment room where the security camera monitors were located.

Arthur was showing Preston the camera angles from different locations. He rose from his seat when Wyatt and Joe entered. "Sergeant Major Magnus, pleasure to meet you." Salazar stuck out his hand and gave Wyatt a firm handshake. "Always good to meet another grunt."

"Prior service?" Wyatt asked.

"Retired after twenty years, four deployments and a lot of nagging from *mi esposa*." Arthur smiled.

"Joe, this is Preston Jones, the man in charge of the contract security staff." Wyatt turned to Preston. "Preston, this is Joe Goodman, he'll be in charge of the dogs."

Joe held out his hand.

As Preston raised his, Bacchus growled and Preston snatched his hand back.

"Sit," Joe commanded, shaking his head. "Sorry about that. He's normally behaved."

"I never cared for dogs," Preston said. "I was bit as a kid."

"Bacchus can sense hesitation. He's one of my best." Joe patted the dog's head.

Bacchus looked up at him, tongue lolling as if he didn't have a mean bone in his body.

"Nice to meet you, Joe." Arthur shook Joe's hand and turned to Wyatt. "Who did you piss off to get this assignment?"

Wyatt shook his head. "I was in the neighborhood and got tapped before I could get out." He glanced around the room. "Nice set up."

Arthur's chest puffed out. "We just upgraded for the big auto show the McCanns staged here."

Joe leaned close. "The McCanns are the biggest name in auto dealerships in San Antonio. Loaded."

Based on the shiny new computer display spread out before them, the McCann money had gone to good use. "Nice."

Arthur turned back to the monitors. "I was showing Preston how far the cameras reach."

"Any blind spots on the outside?" Wyatt asked.

Arthur pointed to the map of the building on the wall. "Here and here. We always position convention center guards at each of these locations as well as at the doors and loading ramps."

"Joe and I would like access and a thorough tour of the facility tomorrow to clear it before the vendors and dignitaries arrive."

Arthur nodded. "I can be here to unlock whatever doors you need. We have nothing to hide here."

"Good, though it's not what you're hiding that I would have issue with." Wyatt glanced at his watch. "I understand there is a social event scheduled for tomorrow night to kick off the convention."

"It's at the hotel," Preston corrected. "Nineteen hundred, sharp. The caterers will be arriving between four and five."

Wyatt nodded, glad Preston was on the ball. From the itinerary Fiona had provided, he'd known the reception would be at the hotel. He was testing Preston to see if he had his ducks in a row. "I'll be at the hotel early to make sure everything is squared away."

"That really won't be necessary," Preston said. "I'll have my people briefed and in place. The metal detectors are being installed as we speak and I have sufficient staff to augment the hotel staff."

"Thank you." Wyatt nodded. "I'll be there anyway."

Preston's lips pressed together. "It will be overkill with two chiefs."

Wyatt glanced at Arthur. "Do you feel like it's overkill?"

Arthur shook his head. "Never when lives are at stake. And the threat level is heightened to orange. With all those foreign dignitaries arriving, the convention goers will be ripe for an attack."

"I don't know why Ms. Allen hired me to provide security for the event if she was going to have someone else take charge," Preston groused. "So be it." He smiled and waved toward the door. "Let's get through this tour so that I can make my personnel assignments. Some of us have more work to do."

Wyatt spent the first part of the afternoon with Arthur and Preston combing over the convention center, meeting with the permanent staff and the men Preston had brought in to take the first shift that evening.

Joe stuck with him throughout the inspection, noting the best places to run his canines through to check for bombs. Bacchus had been eager to set his nose to the task and would have inspected the entire building by himself if Joe had the time to do a thorough sweep.

As they returned to the front entrance, Arthur and Preston stood to one side, talking about camera angles. Joe was telling Wyatt more about the animals he'd bring the next day when a flash of red hair caught Wyatt's attention.

Fiona stood with a man in a maintenance uniform pointing at the lights in the ceiling.

"Wyatt, have you heard anything I've said?"

A hand waved in Wyatt's face and he turned to stare at Joe as if he'd just noticed him. "I'm sorry, what were you saying?"

"You completely zoned out there for a minute."

Wyatt's gaze didn't remain on Joe long. Not when Fiona was so near and gorgeous in her soft gray pencil skirt and orange sherbet blouse.

The wolf whistle next to him yanked him back to Joe.

"Who's the babe?" Joe asked.

His brows furrowing, Wyatt shot a narrowed glance at Joe. "That's our fearless leader, Ms. Fiona Allen." The woman he'd be sleeping with in a couple hours if he could convince her it was a good idea.

"This gig just got better." Joe clapped his hands together and took off toward her, glancing back at Wyatt. "Aren't you coming? On second thought, don't. You'll cramp my style."

Wyatt loped to catch up as Joe stuck out his hand to Fiona. "Joseph Goodman."

Fiona turned a full, captivating smile on him and her entire face lit up.

Someone could have punched him in the gut the way the air left his chest and he couldn't seem to bring any back in.

"Wow. You're really pretty," Joe said, holding her hand longer than was necessary.

Her smile widened and her cheeks flushed. "Well, aren't you the charmer?"

A stab of something that felt oddly like jealousy knifed through Wyatt's heart. What the hell? She hadn't made any promises. She wasn't his to be jealous about. One kiss did not mean she'd committed herself to him, or him to her.

Then why did he feel like beating his chest like a gorilla and then pounding his friend into a pulp for holding Fiona's hand longer than was necessary for a friendly greeting?

"Joe here was about to leave. Weren't you, Joe?" Wyatt gripped his friend's elbow and tried to steer him away from Fiona.

Bacchus growled and bared wickedly sharp teeth.

Wyatt dropped Joe's arm and Fiona backed away, her eyes widening.

"Heel," Joe said. "Don't worry, Ms. Fiona. He won't hurt you. He must think Wyatt's being too aggressive. Bacchus is very sensitive and picks up on others' emotions." Joe smiled at Wyatt, though the smile was a bit forced. "I'd love to talk to you more about the sweep I plan to do with the dogs tomorrow. Do you have plans for dinner?"

"As a matter of fact, she does." Wyatt stepped up beside Fiona and faced Joe. "She's having dinner with me."

Fiona's brows rose high on her forehead. "I am?"

"Yes. Of course you are. We need to go over the details of the convention center security and talk about the hotel."

"That's an excellent idea." Fiona gave him a brilliant smile that made his insides flip. "It would be a great opportunity to put our heads together and get security of our convention goers nailed down so that we don't have any

73

international incidents." She turned to Preston, Joe and Arthur. "Of course we'd need the whole team in on the discussion. Would you three please join us for dinner? I'll also have my assistant attend."

Wyatt's stomach dipped. Dinner with a crowd was not what he had in mind. He tried to make eye contact with Joe to let him know he didn't want him to accept the invitation.

The man didn't even look his way. "I'd love to." Joe grinned like a fool, making Wyatt want to knock all his teeth out. "We can talk through my plans to run the dogs through the convention center."

Preston glanced at his watch. "I can come for a little while, but I have to coordinate with my team before the morning."

Wyatt watched his chances to woo the pretty Fiona slipping through his fingers. He'd hoped to get to know her, and let her get to know him a little better before they slept in the same room, and hopefully in the same bed.

Fiona clapped her hands. "Well, good. It's all set then." She glanced at the clock on her cell phone. "If we could meet at the hotel at seven o'clock, we can find someplace to eat along the River Walk."

"I'll be there," Joe said a little too eagerly.

Wyatt refrained from elbowing him in the gut...just barely.

Preston nodded. "Seven o'clock. If you'll excuse me, I have work to do before tomorrow." The man hurried off.

"I'd better get back to the video display room." Arthur shook Fiona's hand. "I'll have to check with *mi esposa* before I commit to dinner tonight. I'll let you know."

"I have work to do as well. Since the governor couldn't get here on time, I'm greeting the Mexican Prime Minister at the airport in less than an hour." Fiona smiled at Joe, not Wyatt. "I'll see you two tonight."

When she'd gone, Wyatt glared at his friend.

Joe's eyes widened. "What?"

"I meant to have dinner with her. Alone."

A chuckle rumbled in Joe's chest and then grew into a full-bellied laugh. "I loved the look on her face when you announced you were having dinner with her." He rubbed tears from his eyes. "There is no secret to getting a woman to go out with you. You *do* have to ask, not assume she'll agree. You're lucky she didn't throw it back in your face."

"Seems as though she did. And I would have asked, but I've had a lot on my mind."

"If you want to make points with Fiona, you'd better have her as your main focus."

Oh, he did. That was the problem.

"Look, if you want me to back off, say the word." Joe held his hands out, palms up. "I'll tell her I have a sick dog and can't make dinner."

"No. Preston will be there and I'll be damned if I have to make conversation with him. He's pretty tight-lipped."

"I noticed. Should be an interesting evening." Joe continued to smile. "That Fiona is one hot cookie."

"She's not a cookie." Although she was very hot.

"I know, but it's really fun pushing your buttons."

Wyatt crossed his arms. "If we're done here, I'd like you to check out the hotel where most of the dignitaries are staying, including me. If anyone is going to target a building, it'll be the hotel or the convention center." He didn't add that he'd be staying in the same room with Fiona. Joe didn't need to know that.

"You really think someone will try something big?"

"In this day, when terrorists bomb marathons and fly planes into buildings, I wouldn't be surprised by anything." He started toward the parking lot and turned back to his friend. "You coming?"

"Yeah." Joe hurried to catch up, Bacchus trotting at his side.

Wyatt spent the rest of the afternoon going over every entrance to the hotel, the security that was in place, and reviewing the camera angles and identifying blind spots in both the electronic surveillance and the personnel assigned as security guards. The hotel had only token security. Wyatt made a note to talk to Fiona and Preston about his plans to beef up the security staff. At least he'd have something to talk about at the dinner table with Joe, Arthur, Preston and Fiona.

The only thing keeping him going all day was the thought of sharing a room with Fiona that night. He'd have to bone up on his seduction skills. Fiona would suffer no fools. If he wanted to get inside her panties, he'd have only one shot at it. He was damned if he'd blow it.

Fiona was a spitfire with attitude and determination. She'd let nothing stand in the way of making the convention a success. Even him.

After meeting the Mexican delegate at the airport, and a long afternoon of drinking cocktails in the barroom of the hotel, Fiona was counting the minutes until she could escape to her room and take a long, hot bubble bath. By the time she could get away, it was nearing six o'clock.

Hurrying to the elevator, she passed Wyatt with a towel slung around his neck, wearing shorts and flip-flops, probably on his way to the pool or sauna.

Perfect.

She hustled up to the room, showered and changed in record time, half expecting Wyatt to walk in naked like he had before. Her heart rattled in her chest, leaping at every sound.

Rather than get caught nude again, she'd brought all her clothing into the bathroom and dressed there. Every noise, every bump or thump, she jumped and peeked out the door.

Wyatt had yet to return.

By the time she was dressed, her nerves were hopping and she could barely catch her breath. What was wrong with her?

Her hair in place, her makeup just right and having spent as long as she could in the room before heading for the lobby, Fiona finally gave up at a quarter to the hour. Dressed in a slim-fitting pastel green tank-dress that hugged every inch of her body like a glove, she slipped into high-heeled strappy sandals that emphasized her tight calves. She looked more confident than she felt as she headed for the elevator.

When the lift car arrived at her floor, her breath caught and she waited. The door slid open to an empty car. The air left her lungs in a whoosh.

Where the hell was Wyatt? He'd be late if he didn't get a move on. Then again, good. She wouldn't wait, if he didn't show up by seven then she wouldn't have to sit across from him, wondering what it would be like sleeping in the same room with him later that night.

Yeah, right. That thought had been on her mind all day to the exclusion of all else. She didn't have time to daydream about a man. She needed focus.

Fiona checked at the front desk to see which of the delegates had arrived, marking them off the list she kept on her cell phone. So far everyone who was supposed to arrive by now had.

With five minutes to spare, she stepped into the lobby.

It was D minus twenty-four. The kickoff started at seven o'clock the following evening with all the major players for this convention milling around, meeting, greeting and networking. Everything had to go exactly as planned. No hiccups. No distractions. No security issues and no thinking about Wyatt Magnus sleeping in the nude.

There she went again. Fiona closed her eyes, drew in a deep breath and let it out slowly.

"Thinking about me?" a warm deep voice whispered against her ear, melting her like chocolate in the hot Texas sun.

For a moment Fiona leaned toward Wyatt until she realized what she was doing. She pulled herself together and faced him with her best, no-nonsense poker face. "Of course not." She frowned. "Weren't you just in the sauna?" Her gaze swept his length.

His hair was damp and his clothes were clean and dry. And he was as sexy in khaki slacks and a polo shirt as he was in shorts. *Damn the man.*

Wyatt grinned. "I brought my clothes and showered down there to give you some space."

"Oh." She blinked, pleased at his thoughtfulness and at the same time, a little disappointed. The latter emotion surprised her. She shook it off and got down to business. "I'm going over the itinerary of the next twenty-four hours."

"Including who gets the bathroom first tonight?" A grin lifted the corners of his mouth. "I don't even know if you snore."

"That's it." She started toward the reception desk. "I can't do this."

"Wait." He snagged her arm. "I checked before I hit the sauna. They were scrambling to figure out where they're going to put the other double-booked guests. I promise, I'll behave. You won't even know I'm in the room. And as far as I know, I don't snore. We'll be okay. Scout's honor."

She gave him a narrow-eyes look. "Were you even a scout?"

"As a matter of fact, yes." He grinned. "My father made me join to keep me off the streets. I was a very active child and he saw what kind of trouble I could be at an early age."

"I can see that." She sighed. "Very well. Looks like we're stuck with each other. But understand this, I have too much riding on the convention. I don't need any distractions."

He raised his hands. "I wouldn't dream of distracting you."

Yeah well, you already are. Fiona bit down on her tongue to keep from saying it out loud.

"Fiona, there you are." Maddie, dressed in a summery, floral dress in soft pink, yellow and green, hurried through the front door of the hotel. "I thought I was going to be late." When she spied Wyatt, her eyes widened. "Well, well, who do we have here?"

Fiona's teeth ground together as Maddie's gaze swept Wyatt's length from gorgeous brown eyes down to the tip of his cowboy boots.

"Maddie Wells, meet Master Sergeant Wyatt Magnus, on loan from the Army to Homeland Security. He's been placed in charge of the security of this convention." After making the introduction, Fiona held her breath, waiting for Maddie to gush.

Wyatt took Maddie's hand and lifted it to his lips. "The pleasure is mine." He winked at Fiona as he pressed his lips to her assistant's fingers.

A pretty, rosy blush rose up Maddie's neck into her cheeks. "You didn't tell me he was so handsome and charming."

"I can be, when I want to." He straightened, holding Maddie's hand far longer than Fiona deemed necessary.

Her chest tight with a flare of unbidden anger, Fiona stepped out to greet Preston and Joe as they entered the hotel lobby.

"Preston, Joe, glad you made it. Arthur called and said his wife had plans for him, so he won't be joining us. Shall we go find a place to eat?" She hooked her arm through Joe's and stepped through the doors leading directly out onto the River Walk.

Preston, Maddie and Wyatt followed.

Fiona tried not to think about Wyatt behind her. But the nape of her neck tingled as if she could feel his gaze on her backside. She hoped her dress wasn't hitched up in her panties. And if she put a little more sway in her hips, she chalked it up to the high-heeled, strappy sandals. They almost always made her walk like a model on the runway, one foot in front of the other.

They settled on one of the Tex-Mex restaurants with patio seating overlooking the river and a band playing an eclectic mixture of Latin American and soft rock music in the corner by the bar. As the sun set, the twinkle lights adorning the trees and bridges along the River Walk blinked to life. With the soft lighting, the background music and the warm summer night, it would have been a perfect evening for a romantic dinner for two. Glancing across the table, Fiona caught Wyatt's gaze on her. A perfect evening for two *if* she wasn't working through dinner, and *if* she didn't have a convention to keep on track.

After everyone had placed an order, Fiona pulled out her work tablet and started the discussion. "Are we set for tomorrow?" Without waiting for a response, she turned to Joe. "The dogs will start through the convention center at nine in the morning, complete by two in the afternoon, at which time you'll bring them to the hotel."

Joe smiled. "That sounds about right."

Wyatt turned to the supervisor of the hired security team. "Preston already has people in place, augmenting the convention center permanent staff."

Preston nodded. "I'll have additional staff at the entrances when the vendors arrive tomorrow and the day the convention starts. I'll also have eight of my personnel at the function tomorrow night. They will be dressed as wait staff or businessmen, to keep it from appearing too obvious."

Fiona stared down at her tablet, her list of notes blurring as she internalized the schedule. "The meet-and-greet is at seven o'clock tomorrow night. Maddie, you and I will arrive in the hotel ballroom an hour early and stay until the last person leaves."

"Got it, boss." Maddie gave her a mock salute.

"Which leaves you." Fiona stared across at Wyatt. "Mr. Magnus, what exactly will you be doing during all this time?"

Wyatt's eyebrows dipped and then smoothed. "I'll be looking for weaknesses." His lips tilted upward on the corners. "And you?"

A shiver of excitement rippled across her. She had to swallow hard to loosen her vocal cords. "I'll be circulating through the meet-and-greet and then through the convention center the next day. Some of the delegates have a known propensity for drama. I want to curtail any scenes before the press gets wind of it."

"You can't be everywhere at once," Joe said.

Fiona nodded. "Precisely. That's why Maddie will be assisting me in circulating. Each one of us will be equipped with a radio headset. If anything happens, we'll be able to call on each other immediately." She smiled at Joe. "I'm not certain you'll be there throughout, but if you are, you will be rigged with radio communications as well."

"I wouldn't miss it for the world." Joe grinned at Wyatt. "It'll be like on active duty, only our teammates will be dressed to the nines, not covered in sand and smelling like last week's sweat socks."

Maddie turned to Joe. "What branch of service, Joe?"

"Army Special Forces." His chest puffed out. "Three tours to the sandbox, and I was lucky enough to live to tell about it."

Wyatt's jaw tightened as his gaze rested on his friend.

"What about you, Preston?" Fiona turned her attention to the man beside her. "I understand you are prior service."

Preston's gaze narrowed. "Yeah."

"What branch?" she pressed.

"Marine Corps," he answered, his voice clipped, a frown settling between his brows. The man obviously didn't want to talk about it.

Fiona smiled. "My stepfather was in the Marines for twenty-six years. He always said it was the toughest job you'll ever love."

Preston sat in stony silence.

"Wyatt?" Maddie piped in. "What's your background?"

Yeah, Wyatt? What makes you so intense and sexual? Fiona wanted to ask, but she remained quiet, awaiting the man's response.

Wyatt seemed to be working through his answer in his head. "Army," he finally spit out.

Joe chuckled. "Don't let him kid you. He's one of the most decorated soldiers you'll ever meet. He saved my butt a time or two."

Wyatt shrugged. "So, I assume you'll want to meet at the hotel when the dogs have made their sweep?"

Fiona recognized the diversionary tactic and let Wyatt have it. "I'm spending my morning at the convention center and from noon on, I'll be at the hotel managing the details for the evening's event. Find me when you get there. I'd like to hear what you think are the soft spots for security."

The food arrived, thus ending the business portion of the meeting.

After the waiter removed the plates, Fiona ordered a frozen margarita and sat back to enjoy the music and the soft-scented breeze.

The band struck up a song with a lively beat.

Maddie leaped to her feet. "Come on, Wyatt, the music is moving me."

Wyatt shook his head. "I'm too full."

She planted her hands on her hips. "In my neck of the woods, you don't turn down a lady's offer to dance."

"You're right." Wyatt pushed to his feet with a smile. "Forgive my rudeness."

Maddie batted her eyes and hooked her arm through his. "Forgiven. Now show me how well you move those sexy hips." She danced him to the center of the floor and spun to face him, holding out her arms. He spun her into his embrace and moved around the floor like he was built to dance.

"Magnus was always good on the dance floor." Joe stood. "If you don't mind your toes being stepped on, I'd be honored if you'd join me."

Fiona hesitated, not liking to leave a man alone at their table.

Preston settled it by standing as well. "If you'll excuse me, I need to brief my staff one more time and then hit the rack. I'll be up before dawn and would like to be rested."

Shaking his hand, Fiona bid Preston goodnight and took Joe's hand, allowing him to lead her onto the small dance floor. She hadn't danced since college. Busy getting her business up and running, she'd forgone the young social scene.

It felt good to sway to the music. For what Joe lacked in rhythm, he made up for with enthusiasm. By the time the song ended, Fiona was breathless and smiling. If her eyes drifted over to where Wyatt and Maddie were dancing, she didn't let it spoil her fun.

The band shifted to a soft and sensuous salsa. Joe tried a few steps with Fiona leading, but he laughed and gave up.

"Trade ya," Maddie said, appearing beside Fiona with Wyatt on her arm. "I think I can teach Joe a few tricks."

Wyatt held out his hand.

With a sense of excitement mixed with dread, Fiona placed her hand in his palm and let him draw her into his arms.

They fit together all too well, his hips rocking her hips in time to the music. Joe had been right, Wyatt could dance. A man who was strong, ruggedly good looking and could dance was a triple threat to Fiona. He reminded her just how much she loved to dance and made her wonder why she'd given it up for the sake of her career.

At the same time, being so close to Wyatt only made her infinitely more aware of his hard muscles, thick thighs and massive arms. How would it feel to be naked, her soft breasts pressed against his rock-hard muscles again? For a moment she melted against him, ready to feel the next best thing. When she realized just how close she was, she stiffened and tried to draw away.

His hand on the small of her back held her in place. "Loosen up," Wyatt whispered into her ear. "Feel the music and let me show you how to move."

"I know how to dance," she retorted, though her voice sounded weak.

"Then show me." He spun her around, his thigh pushing between hers, his hand creeping lower down her back, pressing her against the solid ridge beneath his fly.

Angry that he thought she couldn't hold her own on the dance floor and even angrier at herself for caring, she closed her eyes and gave herself up to the music. As far as she was concerned, she could be with any man and still dance the same.

He twirled her away then back into his arms, his body rubbing hers from his chin to his calves, inciting a riot with her nervous system.

Holy hell, her body was on fire, raging with need to be with him…in bed…alone, not surrounded by a crowd of vacationing tourists.

Nearing the end of the passion-filled song, Wyatt swept her up against him and bent her backwards, exposing her throat.

When the music ended, he held her still, bent over her, his lips so close she could feel the warmth of his breath. Just a half-inch would close the distance.

"Uh, Fiona, dear," Maddie said beside her. "The music stopped."

Fiona stared up into Wyatt's eyes and blinked, the moment gone.

Wyatt set her on her feet. "Thank you for the dance."

Brushing her hands down the length of the dress, she pushed her hair back from her face. "Well, I should call it a ni—"

A loud crash from the direction of the kitchen made everyone jump.

Wyatt grabbed her around the middle, shoved her to the floor and threw himself on top of her.

Crushed to the sticky tiles, Fiona could barely breathe, much less move beneath the weight and strength of the man above her.

"Magnus," Joe spoke, as if from a distance. "It's okay. The bus boy dropped a tub of dishes. It's okay." He grabbed Wyatt's elbow and dragged him to his feet.

Unfettered by Wyatt's big body, Fiona rolled to her feet and studied the man.

His face was pale, his brows dipped into a fierce frown, his hands bunched into fists. "Have to go."

"Magnus. It's okay," Joe repeated. "The reflex will fade. You just have to give it time."

Wyatt turned to Fiona, his gaze sweeping over her rumpled, stained dress, his jaw twitching on the side. "I'm sorry." He tossed some bills on the table, pushed through the throng of people staring at him and left the restaurant.

Fiona shook her head. "What the hell just happened?"

Joe stared after his friend. "PTSD. Post Traumatic Stress Disorder."

"And that makes him throw women to the ground?"

Joe smiled sadly. "He'd have thrown me to the ground had I been closest to him." He shook his head. "It's been the hardest thing for me to deal with since my last deployment. An IED exploded next to my HMMWV. Rattled my brain and I can't sit still too long. I get punchy. I think Wyatt had it worse."

"How so?" Fiona's gaze followed Wyatt as he took off along the sidewalk bordering the River Walk. She wanted to go after him but knew she couldn't keep up. Not in heels.

"From what I heard, Wyatt was captured and tortured on his last mission. I don't know what all they did to him, but it must have been bad. That's why he's here in San Antonio. He just recently was released from the hospital."

Maddie touched her arm. "Are you okay, Fiona?"

She nodded. "Yes, I'm just a little tired. I think I'll head back to my room."

"I'll see Maddie to the parking garage," Joe offered.

Stunned by Wyatt's action and abrupt departure, she nodded absently and said, "Thanks. See you two tomorrow." She left the restaurant. Instead of heading straight for the hotel, she turned the direction Wyatt had gone.

After walking for several blocks, her feet hurt in the heels and she wished she'd had on her jogging shorts and tennis shoes. Catching up to Wyatt would be impossible, even if she knew which direction he'd gone.

Her heart heavy, she turned back and arrived at the hotel before ten o'clock.

The lobby was busy with guests checking in late. Many spoke other languages and had an entourage of staff with them.

Though she felt as if she should be greeting them and making them feel welcome, Fiona didn't have it in her to be sociable. The thought of a tortured Wyatt roaming the streets of San Antonio bothered her more than she would have expected.

She took the elevator up and let herself into the room she'd share with Wyatt...if he returned. As she swiped her card through the locking mechanism, she held her breath, praying he'd be inside, safe and sound.

Pushing the door open, she let go of the breath she'd held. No Wyatt. The room was cold and empty, much like her life had been up to the point at which she'd been bumped into the river and pulled out by a big strapping soldier.

Without bothering to duck into the bathroom, Fiona stripped out of her sandals and dress and pulled her nightgown over her head. The blue baby-doll, sheer gown barely came down over her bottom. If she'd known she'd be sharing a room, she might have brought pajamas that covered her from neck to toe. Not knowing if the AC would be sufficient to keep her cool, she'd chosen the lightest gown she had. If she hadn't been crazy busy all day, she'd have gone home to get less revealing PJs. Or she could have asked Maddie to stop by her place, but she'd sent her off on other more pressing matters than PJs.

Too tired and dispirited to worry about it, she fluffed her pillow, climbed into the bed and leaned back against the headboard, sitting up, waiting for Wyatt to return to their room.

Worry kept her awake past midnight. Despite the activities of the day, she couldn't force her eyelids closed. Instead she slipped down into the sheets, afraid to go to sleep for fear of dreaming of the man who'd thrown her on the floor to protect her from attack.

After an hour of lying there, staring at the ceiling, wondering what had set the man off, she climbed out of the bed and wandered into the bathroom. A shower might clear her head and let her finally get to sleep. Stripping out of her nightgown, she climbed into the tub and turned on the shower. Cool water to chill the desire rising in her every time her mind drifted back to the soldier who'd be sleeping in her room. Should she let him into her bed to get him out of her system? Or should she keep to her plan and remain abstinent throughout the conference?

Fiona switched the water colder until she was shivering by the time she stepped out of the shower and still her body warmed from the inside.

Damn the man for invading her thoughts when he wasn't even there for her to do anything about.

Chapter Six

Wyatt walked to the end of the River Walk and out into the streets of downtown San Antonio with no direction in mind, just the need to move and keep moving. He felt as if he stopped, his demons would catch up to him and take him down, and he couldn't give in.

Every loud noise made him jumpy and jittery. The more he reacted, the more sensitive he became to noises, hearing even the slightest sounds like he had when he'd been working his way door-to-door in a poor Somali village, searching for the rogue warriors. When he couldn't take it any longer, he slipped into a seedy bar and ordered a whiskey.

One drink would take the edge off. If he let himself, he could drown himself to the point he no longer felt the pain. Alcohol also allowed him to fall into a drunken stupor and sleep until morning without the horrific nightmares that plagued him every time he closed his eyes.

A redhead with brilliant green eyes kept him from going down the slick path of alcoholic oblivion. She had a plan and he'd by God better toe the line. Showing up for work drunk or hung over was never a good idea when terrorists had already threatened. Thirty minutes, maybe an hour had passed. He wasn't sure. He would have liked to say he didn't care as he stared into the glass of amber liquid he had yet to touch.

Those damned green eyes haunted him and he could almost imagine the disappointment in them if he didn't take the job seriously and show up for work. His troubles were insignificant. People's lives depended on him being one step ahead of terrorists. Like in Somalia. Only he hadn't been far enough ahead to keep his friend from dying. Maybe, just maybe, he could make a difference this time. But not numbed by alcohol.

He pushed the untouched glass away, slapped a twenty on the counter and left the bar. At a slow jog, he took only fifteen minutes to find his way back to the hotel, ignoring the ache in his knee. He wouldn't forgive himself if something happened while he was away feeling sorry for himself.

Wyatt entered the lobby, his strides eating up the distance between him and the elevator. He hit the sublevel that led to the parking garage and the security office with the camera monitors. After checking with the security guard on duty and giving him his cell phone number, Wyatt returned to the elevator, his heartbeat quickening as the car lifted to the floor with the room he'd share with Fiona.

Fingering the keycard in his pocket, he wondered if she'd managed to convince the concierge to change the lock code on the door to make his key card obsolete. He half expected the lock indicator light to blink red when he slid his card in the reader.

Ready to turn and walk away, he was surprised to see the light blink green. He gripped the handle and pushed the door, once again expecting the chain to block his entry.

When the door swung open, he stepped into the darkened room and nearly ran into the rollaway someone must have set up in his absence. Neatly made up with sheets, a blanket and pillow, it stood as far away as it could possibly get from the bed where Fiona would be sleeping. The only light shining from the base of the bathroom door barely provided enough light for Wyatt to locate the king-sized bed. The whir of a blow dryer came to an abrupt stop.

Wyatt let the door close behind him. He eased his way around the cot, shedding his shirt and shoes.

The light in the bathroom blinked out, plunging him into complete darkness, the heavy, light-smothering curtains across the window disallowing any streetlight to penetrate the room.

The soft sound of a metal doorknob twisting and the barely discernible creak of hinges let him know Fiona was done in the bathroom and headed for the king-sized bed.

A soft thump was followed by a muttered curse. "Damn."

Wyatt inched forward, concerned she'd hurt herself, but afraid he'd run into her if he hurried.

He hadn't gone far when, the light from the bathroom flickered on and Fiona was silhouetted, wearing a short, baby-doll nightgown, the shape of her body clearly visible through the diaphanous fabric.

Standing only inches from her, Wyatt's pulse quickened. He could barely see the expression on her face, but her quick indrawn breath let him know she'd seen him.

"Oh," she said, pressing a hand to the gentle swell of her breasts. "I didn't hear you come in."

"I'm not surprised."

She glanced up at him, the light shining off the side of her face, giving it a sexy glow. "I'm done in the bathroom. It's all yours."

"Thank you." He didn't move out of her way. His body warring with his mind. He'd assured her she had nothing to fear from him. That he'd be the perfect gentleman sharing a room with her. But all those promises seemed to fly out the window with her luscious body so close to his, her chest rising and falling in rapid succession, her scent wafting around him like an invitation.

She swiped her tongue across her lips, drawing Wyatt's attention to their full, plump dampness. As much as he didn't trust himself and as much as he didn't want to get involved, he was afraid it was too late. He gripped her arms and stared down into her eyes. "I didn't come here to start something," his voice edged with desperate anger.

"Then don't," she whispered. "No one's making you." She said one thing, her body contradicting her words when she swayed toward him.

"I made a promise," he reminded her.

"I wouldn't want you to break any promises." Fiona's gaze shifted to his naked chest, her hands rising to rest on the muscles. Instead of pushing him away, her fingers curled ever so slightly, her nails grazing his skin. "Then again, sometimes promises are made to be broken."

He dragged in a breath, but the air didn't seem to fill his lungs. Finally, he gave in to his baser desires and bent to claim her lips in a fierce kiss.

Rather than shy away in alarm by his actions, Fiona raised her arms, entwining her hands at the back of his neck, dragging him closer, her barely clad breasts pressing against his naked skin. The nipples puckered into hard little tips grazing him, making him want to rip the gown over her head.

He broke the kiss, trailing his lips over her cheek, down her chin, following the long line of her neck to where it crooked at her shoulder.

She let her head fall back, exposing more skin to his lips and tongue. "Why can't I stop? You're like an addiction." She moaned. "The more I have, the more I want."

Her words ignited a flame so bright it burned through him in seconds, consuming him. He slid his hands down her back and cupped the backs of her thighs, lifting her in his arms and wrapping her legs around his waist. He spun toward the bed and eased her down onto the crisp clean sheets, bending over her, his mouth poised above hers. When she reached out to pull him down on her, he held back, grasping her wrists in his bigger hands, pinning them to the mattress above her head. "You need to know."

"What?" she said, her body writhing beneath his. "That I'm on fire? That I want you?"

His groin tightened, blood flowing south, engorging his cock, making his jeans so tight he might explode. "You need to know I'm not staying. What we're about to do means nothing. I'm no good at relationships. Don't expect me to behave any differently tomorrow. It'll be back to business as usual."

For a moment hurt flashed in her eyes and she lay still, not struggling against his grip on her wrists. Then her lips quirked up on the corner. "Okay, soldier. I'm more than good with that. And I'm glad you clarified, because I don't have time for a clingy man." She arched her back, pressing her breasts against his chest, the smile spreading across her face. "Now, are you going to fuck me, or am I going to have to break out my vibrator?"

The reasoning part of Wyatt's mind flew out the shrouded window and his body shouted *Hallelujah!*

Fiona couldn't believe she'd just given him consent to ravage her body. Then again, she'd been anticipating this since he'd run out on their dinner earlier that evening. Hadn't she been wishing he'd show up? The cool shower forgotten, her body heated like a raging inferno centered around her aching, throbbing core.

Like a conquering warrior, he claimed her lips, his mouth bearing down, his tongue thrusting against hers.

She surrendered gladly, meeting his tongue with her own caresses. She slid her hands along his arms and down his body to cup his ass. Tight denim encased hard muscles, bunching and flexing with each move. Wanting him to lie on the bed beside her, she grasped his buttocks, urging him to climb in.

He resisted, shaking his head as he released her lips. "Not yet. I might be rusty at this, but I like my women to be as excited as I am."

Women. Fiona would have snorted and started to, but Wyatt shifted, his lips sliding down her neck to capture one of her nipples between his teeth. He rolled the hardened bead, dampening the fabric of her gown.

Her back arching as if of its own accord, Fiona fought to breathe.

Then with an impatient movement, Wyatt straightened, gripped the hem of her gown, yanked it up over her head and tossed it over his shoulder.

She sat up and reached for the button of his jeans.

His hand descended over hers. "Not yet," he repeated.

"But I like to make love to my men naked."

His eyes flared, his lips tightening for a moment. "In time. You let him loose and I won't have any control left."

She laughed softly. "And that's a problem?" She yanked the top button free.

Again he stopped her, stepping away from her reach.

Fiona pressed her lips together, frustration lending to her impatience. "Fine. We'll do it your way." She cocked her head to the side, her brows rising in challenge.

He met her challenge by slipping a finger beneath the elastic of her panties.

Thankful she'd worn her best black lace thong, she watched as he slid the scrap of fabric over her hips and down her legs excruciatingly slowly.

By the time he yanked them free, she was all but panting. Her pussy creamed when he stepped between her knees. Still sitting up, she ran her hands over his chest and downward over his ripped belly. "Don't make me wait too long."

His lips hovering over the pulse beating at the base of her neck, he breathed warm air across her skin. "I'll make it worth your time."

"I'm counting on it." She ran her hands over her breasts, plumping them for his pleasure and then let her fingers slide down to the tuft of hair covering her sex. Parting her folds, she fingered her clit, slipping lower to coat a digit in the liquid seeping from her channel. He just wasn't moving fast enough for her. She needed him inside her. Sooner rather than later.

When he dropped to his knees, her heart seized and she stroked her clit faster. In all the relationships she'd been in, and there hadn't been many, never once had a man gone down on her. She shivered, her knees widening to accommodate his broad shoulders brushing against the insides of her thighs.

He reached out, lifting her breasts in the palms of his hands, rolling the nipples between his thumbs and forefingers. "You have beautiful breasts."

Fiona had always considered them nothing more than adequate. But the hunger in Wyatt's gaze made her want to believe him. She cupped the backs of his hands and squeezed his fingers around them.

After a moment, he dragged his hands away from beneath hers and caressed her sides, leaning in to capture a turgid peak between his lips.

Fiona drew in a deep breath, her chest pushing out to meet his lips and offer more.

He sucked her nipple into his mouth, pulling hard.

Her insides tightened and she threaded her hands through his hair, cupping the back of his skull to bring him nearer.

Ah, yes. She liked the way he sucked hard, the slight pain stimulating everything else in her body to a heightened sense of awareness. It only made her want more.

He abandoned her breasts and eased his way down her torso to the tiny triangle of hair at the apex of her thighs. Glad she'd had a bikini wax the day before, she waited, holding her breath for what came next.

Wyatt glanced up. "Tell me to stop and I will."

"Fuck no, you won't," she wailed. "Please, don't stop now." Fiona threaded her fingers through his hair and urged him on his path downward.

Streamers of electric shocks rippled through her as his fingers parted her folds, laying open her clit for the next stage in his calculated attack.

He flicked the slim bit of flesh with the tip of his tongue.

Fiona's fingers dug into his scalp, a moan rising from her chest, escaping through parted lips, air lodging in her throat.

He chuckled, his breath cooling the dampened skin. Before she could catch her breath, he stroked her again with that magical tongue.

Her head fell back, her hands trembling.

Two strokes and she was ready to beg him to take her, fuck her, slam into her hard and fast.

Instead, he pulled her clit into his mouth and nibbled gently, swirling his tongue around it until every one of the tightly packed nerves were screaming with delight.

When he dipped a finger into her channel, she almost launched off the bed. Two fingers were even better. Three fingers, plus the continuous flicking, sucking and tapping at her clit sent her flying over the edge. "Now," she begged. "Please come inside me now."

He lurched to his feet, scooted her up on the bed and dug into the back pocket of his discarded jeans for his wallet, from which he extracted a foil packet.

Desperate to have him inside her, Fiona sat up and reached for the condom.

Naked, standing in front of her, his cock jutted out, thick, hard and so big it made Fiona's mouth water. Tearing the foil packet open with her teeth, she held off removing it from the pouch, tempted to taste him as he'd tasted her.

She slipped off the bed to kneel at his feet and wrapped her hands around his length. Velvet-encased steel. He thrust into her palms.

Flicking her tongue across the tip, she reveled in the warm, softness. Now that she was there, she wanted to make him as crazy as he'd made her. She laid the condom packet on the pillow beside her, slipped her fingers down to the base of his cock and cupped his balls in her palms.

His quickly indrawn breath and stiffened body told her she was on the right track.

Emboldened, she leaned forward and traced the rim with the tip of her tongue, sliding across the top to dip into the tiny hole.

His dick pulsing, Wyatt dug his fingers in her hair and urged her to take him.

Fiona opened her mouth, wrapping her lips around the bulbous tip.

He flexed his hips, thrusting into her.

She didn't object, adjusting to take his full length until it bumped into the back of her throat, liking the way it made her feel. Though at his feet, she felt the power of what she was doing to him and settled into a smooth rhythm, sucking him in and easing back off. Pressure of his hand in her hair let her know when to speed up, until he grew so stiff, he jerked out of her mouth, scooped her into his arms and tossed her onto the bed.

Like a marauding soldier, he climbed up between her legs, took the condom from the pillow beside her and rolled it down over his damp cock. Then he flipped her onto her belly, raising her hips until her ass poked into the air.

Too excited to protest, she noted another first. She'd never made love doggy-style. Now she wondered why. It was so deliciously primal, animalistic and hotter than hell. Exposed and loving it, she curled her hands into the sheets as Wyatt thrust into her, burying himself all the way to the hilt.

Her channel clenched around him as he dragged himself back out and thrust into her again. He rode her like a bucking bronco, slapping her ass every other thrust. The sting of his hand raising her pleasure another notch.

Fiona rocketed into the stratosphere, her body jerking with the force of her orgasm.

Wyatt thrust into her once more, then bent over her, cupping her breasts, his cock sunk deep inside, throbbing, pulsing in rhythm with her.

Her arms trembling, Fiona collapsed onto the bed, Wyatt following her down. For a moment she couldn't find the strength to do more than moan, which she did.

Wyatt pulled free of her and removed the spent condom, dropping it in the waste basket beside the bed. He rolled over onto his side, turning her over to face him. He brushed the hair out of her face and skimmed his thumb over her swollen lips. "Are you all right?"

"Holy shit," she breathed, touching his thumb with her tongue. "Are you always that good?"

A chuckle rumbled from his throat. "If I said it was my trademark, would that offend you?"

"Not in the least. I'd understand completely. If you could package that and sell it, millions of women would be standing in line to buy. Including me." She closed her eyes briefly and dragged in a shaky breath. "Wow. I mean, wow." Fiona lay for a moment, hoping her pulse would slow to normal. But with his cock nudging her thigh, she didn't see that happening anytime in the near future. Facing the truth head on, she knew she couldn't be satisfied with one round of sex with the soldier. She curled her fingers around his still stiff cock and squeezed gently. "How long until we can do that again?"

A bark of laughter erupted from his throat and he gathered her close, resting her head in the crook of his arm. "Let me catch my breath, sweetheart. Let me catch my breath."

Chapter Seven

Making love to Fiona the second time was a completely different experience and even more moving than the first. What it lacked in the fierce need of the first coupling, it made up for with the intensity of burning desire and tenderness expressed. Taking his time, he coaxed her to the edge by playing his fingers through her folds, flicking at the swollen nub of flesh between.

When he had her where he wanted her, begging him to fill her, he opted to enter her mission-style, preferring to observe the range of emotions crossing her pretty face as he thrust into her. Her pussy closed around him, tight, hot and drenched in her juices. She wrapped her legs around his waist, digging her heels into his ass.

For a moment, he thought perhaps this was his reward for surviving the hell of captivity in Somalia. As he lay with Fiona gathered in his arms, he could almost imagine a normal life. Waking up in the morning to sweet kisses from a beautiful redhead after making love, followed by a restful night's sleep. A life in which he could lie by his lover's side and forget all the tragedy he'd witnessed, maybe even get past the nightmares that had plagued him since his liberation from the Somali militants.

But he couldn't allow himself to relax in a woman's arms. His dreams had been so violent he'd hurt himself before he could awaken. What would happen to Fiona if he allowed himself to fall victim to the horrific nightmares? Unwilling to risk it, he eased his arm out from under her, pressed a feather-soft kiss to her lips, the simple gesture sparking desire anew. Forcing back his longing, he left her bed.

Too wound up to sleep, he paced until his craving subsided and he could lie still. Stretching out on the rollaway cot, he stared up at the ceiling, longing to crawl back in bed with Fiona.

At one point, she stirred and moaned softly.

Wyatt gave an answering groan and turned away. Until he could control his nightmares, he was no good for Fiona or any other woman. Tomorrow he'd see about getting a different room. The temptations were too powerful while he was alone with her. His mind made up, he drifted into a disturbed slumber, fraught with terrorists lurking in every shadow.

Fiona woke before dawn, the darkness like a black abyss. Something had disturbed her, but with her mind so fogged with sleep, she didn't know what. Reaching out to her side, she felt for the warmth and comfort of her soldier's chiseled body, only to feel the cool sheets against her fingertips. He'd left her bed. Had he left her room?

She lay still, listening for the reassuring sound of his breathing, hoping he snored just a little. A groan sounded on the far side of the room from the direction of the door and the rollaway bed.

The springs creaked and the sheets rustled sharply as if someone fought to be free of them.

"Wyatt?" she called out softly.

The only answer was another ragged groan.

Fiona rolled out of the bed and felt her way along the wall to the bathroom. Leaving the door mostly closed, she flipped the light switch, illuminating the bedroom just enough she could see the man caught in deep sleep, thrashing against the sheets, his naked body covered in sweat.

"Wyatt," Fiona called out. She hurried across the floor and knelt beside him, her gaze skimming across his naked skin, angling lower to the nest of hair at the apex of his thighs. His cock lay flaccid, his fists clenched in the sheets at his side. Whatever he dreamed of caused him so much stress his head twisted back and forth.

"No," he called out. "Don't kill him. Please." His words were mumbled but their meaning clear and the anguish on his sleeping face tore down the walls of any defenses Fiona might have fooled herself into believing were strong enough to resist this man.

Her vocal cords knotted in her throat, she swallowed hard and touched his shoulder lightly.

Wyatt jackknifed in the rollaway bed, caught her hand and yanked her across him, catching her throat in a headlock in the crook of his arm.

Fiona tried to cry out, but the air had been cut off to her lungs. She fought his hold, tearing at his arm with her fingernails. She kicked her heels but barefooted she left little impression on the man caught in the throes of a world only he could see.

As the gray haze crept in the sides of her vision, she stopped struggling. Nothing she could do, no matter how hard she fought would break his hold.

As she allowed her body to go limp, his grip slackened until he let go altogether.

Fiona sucked air into her starving lungs and slipped to the floor, out of his reach, her gaze on him wary, ready to move quickly if the need arose.

Wyatt's eyes were wide open as he stared down at her. He blinked once, his brows drawing together. "Fiona? What are you doing on the floor?"

She gulped hard to clear her throat, her hand pressed to the skin still warm from his arm's lock. "You don't remember?"

He shook his head, his eyes widening. "Oh dear God, did I hurt you?" He dropped to the floor beside her, reaching for her.

Moving out of range of his hands, she shook her head. He didn't remember. He'd been so entrenched in his dream world, he didn't recall grabbing her. "Wyatt, you were dreaming."

He scrubbed his hand through his hair. "I hurt you." He buried his face in his hands for a long moment. "I was afraid of that." He pushed to his feet and turned away.

Fiona rose and started to lay her hand on his back when she noticed the ragged lines of welts crisscrossing his skin. She'd felt them earlier, but had been too overcome by passion to ask. Now that she could see them clearly and feel the raised scars, her chest tightened. "Wyatt, what happened to you?" she asked softly, tracing one of the angry lines.

"Nothing." He shrugged off her touch and reached for his T-shirt, pulling it over his head. Grabbing his jeans, he dragged them up his legs and buttoned them. Then he bent to shove his foot into a boot.

Her heart aching for him, she stepped closer. "Come back to bed," Fiona said, feeling him slipping away from her, the stone wall of silence eating at her.

At first he said nothing as he dragged his jeans down over the boot. "I can't sleep with you, Fiona. I might hurt you again."

She laid a hand on his shoulder.

Wyatt jammed his other foot into the boot and then straightened. "I told you. I'm not the forever kind of guy. I come with far too much baggage. I'll see the concierge about another room. If I can't get one, I'll sleep in my Jeep in the parking garage."

"No." She grabbed his arm. "You can't sleep in parking garage. I'm sure there's some rule to that effect."

"Then I'll sleep out on a park bench. The weather's warm."

"Please." She gripped his elbow. "Please stay with me."

"No. I'll end up hurting you worse than this time." He stepped past her and her hand fell to her side.

"I'm willing to take that risk," she said softly.

He turned to face her. "You might be willing to risk your life. I'm not. I've already lost someone I cared about by not recognizing my limitations. I won't lose another." He looped his shoulder holster over his arm. "Do yourself a favor and stay away from me. I'm bad news."

Fiona could tell by the firm set of his square jaw that there was nothing that she could say that would change his mind. With her heart heavy in her chest, she watched as he left, closing the door with a definitive click behind him.

"You're not bad news," she whispered. "You're the best thing that's happened to me in a long time."

And now he was gone.

Wide awake and hating himself for hurting Fiona, Wyatt channeled his anger into his work. He walked the short distance to the convention center, checking in with the night security guard. The sun had yet to appear over the horizon, but it was on its way, heralded by the gray pre-light of dawn. For the next three hours, he combed the building, checking storerooms, walking every inch of the facility, memorizing the entrances, the staircases and the security camera blind spots. Vendors started arriving and unloading at around seven o'clock, anxious to set up display booths where they'd demonstrate the products or services they had to offer in a free trade market. The flurry of activity increased with each passing hour, the number of trucks coming and going giving Wyatt an uneasy feeling about the security of the building and its occupants.

Joe's team of dogs and handlers arrived at eight o'clock and laid out the plan for checking through the vendor-delivered items and the trucks waiting at the loading docks, as well as making a thorough sweep of the building itself.

Wyatt met Joe at the entrance and shook his hand. "Sorry about running out on you last night."

Joe shrugged. "I know what it's like. Been where you are and still have my moments."

Wyatt swallowed past the lump in his throat. Damned right, Joe knew how it was. He'd been in therapy for over six months. The dogs had been the ticket out. "Thanks."

"Yeah. You didn't hurt my feelings." Joe grinned. "Besides, I got some one-on-one time with the pretty redhead."

Wyatt's hands knotted into fists until he realized Joe was yanking his chain.

"She's feisty that one," Joe said. "I had to hold her back to keep her from going after you." He shot a glance at Wyatt. "Smart, pretty and caring. Three of the things I like most in a woman. You going after her?"

Wyatt shook his head. "I'm not ready."

"Well, if you're not ready, mind if I ask her out?"

"Yes, I mind," he bit out before he could think.

Joe laughed, holding up his hands in surrender. "Okay, okay. I get it. You don't want to stake a claim, but you don't want anyone else poaching on the lady in the meantime." He crossed his arms. "Doesn't quite seem fair, but then I'm not a man to horn in on another man's lover."

Wyatt started to tell Joe that he wasn't Fiona's lover. But then that would be a lie. He'd made love to her the night before. That didn't mean he had any kind of claim on her. He'd told her he didn't want to start something. And he meant it. With his memories so fresh in his mind and the violence of his dreams, he didn't trust himself to sleep with anyone. Especially not Fiona.

"I can see you have some issues to gnaw on." Joe jerked his head to the side. "While you're chewing, let's get this show on the road." He assigned sectors for each handler to manage and sent them on their way with instructions on what to look for and the procedure for if they found anything. When the dogs and handlers had dispersed, Joe tugged on Bacchus's lead. "Come." He glanced at Wyatt. "You're welcome to tag along if you want. Bacchus and I love company."

Wyatt fell in step with Joe and Bacchus as they searched one of the sections of the convention center Wyatt had been through earlier that morning. The dog sniffed and nosed around, moving on without stopping for long. Once they'd completed their sector, Joe guided the dog to the vendor displays in the center of the convention center. One row at a time, they traversed the showroom, noting each display, the items arranged on the tables and the people representing the products. Wyatt had scanned through the list of names and companies. Each entrant had been run through the FBI's watch list before being approved, something Fiona had arranged months in advance of the convention.

Bacchus never once stopped to lie down like he would if someone had packed a bomb among the display setups or swag.

When they'd completed the sweep, Wyatt felt a little more confident about the building and the contents. His stomach rumbled, reminding him he hadn't eaten. "Want to get some breakfast?" he asked Joe. "I'll buy."

"I'm always up for a free meal. Why don't we ask your boss to join us?" He nodded toward the door where a perfectly dressed, prim and proper event planner entered. Her light charcoal skirt and wrinkle-free matching jacket were as neatly put together as the woman wearing them. She wore her deep red hair up and twisted into an elegant knot, pinned to the back of her head, the wild curls tucked in place, exposing the long pale length of her throat.

Wyatt could almost taste her skin. His groin tightened as he recalled every line and curve of the body beneath the skirt and jacket.

Before Wyatt could stop him, Joe raised a hand and called out, "Fiona, over here."

Fiona glanced up and smiled at Joe. When her gaze connected with Wyatt's her smile slipped and a rosy red blush crept up her neck to blossom in her cheeks.

Joe's brows dipped and his lips curled up on the edges. "I didn't know redheads could blush that red." He glanced from Fiona to Wyatt and back. "Damn. You two got it on last night, didn't you?" he said quietly enough only Wyatt would hear.

Wyatt's jaw hardened. "Shut the fuck up."

Fiona crossed the tile floor to where they stood.

Joe's grin broadened and he reached out to shake Fiona's hand. "You look gorgeous as usual, Ms. Fiona."

Her answering smile made Wyatt's cock jerk. "Thank you, Joe."

Joe tilted his head to the side. "Are those shadows I detect beneath your eyes? The convention making you lose sleep?"

Wyatt shoved an elbow into his friend's side. "With as much riding on this event, as well as terrorist threats, I imagine sleepless nights come with the job description."

Fiona gave him a brief smile. "Right. I'll be glad when it's all over and everyone is safely on their way back to their respective countries."

"In the meantime, won't you join us for breakfast?" Joe asked. "Would sure make the scenery a lot brighter than looking across the table at Wyatt's ugly mug."

Even before he'd finished asking, Fiona was shaking her head. "I'm sorry. I have too much to do this morning."

"You should eat to keep your strength up. From what I understand it'll be a very long day, and if I'm not mistaken you probably skipped breakfast." Joe gripped her elbow and led her toward the exit, refusing to take no for an answer.

"Joe, let her be. If she doesn't want to go to breakfast with you, don't push her," Wyatt said.

Fiona wavered. "Well, I could stand a cup of coffee."

"It's settled then." Joe pulled her hand through the crook of his elbow. "You're coming with us."

Wyatt followed behind the two as they walked out into the already warming Texas sunshine. As he trailed the other two, he couldn't avoid noticing the twitch of Fiona's hips and the way her skirt tightened around her thighs with every step she took. Those thighs had been wrapped around his waist at several points during the previous night's mattress gymnastics. They were strong and sexy as hell. The woman worked out. Another thing he liked about her. Hell, there wasn't much he *didn't* like. Which made it even harder to resist her.

His jeans tightened, his cock pressing hard against his zipper. If he could trust Joe not to make a move on Fiona, he'd leave and let them eat breakfast alone. But the thought of Fiona with anyone else but him set his teeth on edge. Which didn't make any sense at all. He didn't want her. No, that wasn't right.

He wanted her more than he wanted his next breath.

Trouble was, he didn't want to hurt her.

Chapter Eight

Fiona sat beside Joe, directly across the table from Wyatt. Though she didn't let her gaze connect with his too often, she could feel him staring at her and it made her squirm in her seat, her thighs tightening, her pussy creaming all over again. She could still feel the warm, wet rasp of his tongue across her clit and the weight of his palms cupping her breasts.

Trying to force her mind out of the bedroom, she picked at the breakfast taco on her plate, her appetite nonexistent.

For food.

What was Joe saying? So deep in her thoughts about being naked with Wyatt, she'd missed half of what he was talking about.

"One of my connections at the local FBI office informed me that they have been getting warnings from Washington to be on the lookout for trouble. The tech gurus in the cyber division say there's been increased activity among known terrorist organizations in connection with the International Trade Convention."

Fiona dragged her attention back to the conversation, the importance of which could be the difference between a successful convention and a complete disaster where delegates and civilians could die. "All the more reason to be on our toes at all times. We don't want anyone hurt." Despite her effort to avoid Wyatt, her gaze rose to his and locked.

His dark brown gaze bore into hers. "No, we don't want anyone hurt."

Joe stared from Fiona to Wyatt. "On that we can all agree. Which makes it all the more imperative to stop situations from happening before they become dangerous."

Wyatt nodded. "Exactly. We should avoid trouble where at all possible. Even if it means denying certain persons from being around others."

"Right." Joe tapped his finger on the table. "I understand the Columbians and the Venezuelans have been calling each other names. Perhaps you should keep the delegates from those two countries out of each other's way."

Fiona stared at Wyatt a moment longer, her brows lifting. Not only would they need to keep certain delegates apart, Wyatt would probably try to maintain his distance from her as well. "The social event tonight will be a challenge. I've studied the list of guests and made notes on who has issues with whom."

"I'd like to have that list," Wyatt said.

"It's in my room at the hotel. If you come two hours before the event, I'll brief you on who to watch out for." She glanced away, fighting to keep her lips from quirking up on the corners. Not only would she brief him on the people attending, but she might even *de*brief him for a little pre-hors d'oeuvre snack before the evening's ordeal.

Oh yeah. He didn't wear briefs. That smile she'd been holding onto broke through. Even better. If the man thought he could make love to her so expertly the night before and walk out of her life the next morning, he had another think coming. So he had some issues with PTSD? She could deal with it. Her parents hadn't raised a wimp.

Her mind made up, her day laid out with so many coordination tasks to tick and tie, she pushed back from the table to get started. "If you'll excuse me, gentlemen, I have work to do." She stared across the table at Wyatt. "I'll see you later."

His eyes narrowed, but he nodded.

As far as Fiona was concerned the day couldn't go fast enough. All the plans she'd made for the convention were falling into place. The caterer was on target to deliver on time, Joe and his dogs would be sweeping the hotel again at noon. Preston would have guards positioned at each entrance and exit, along with one of Joe's bomb-sniffing dogs and handlers. The social event would take place in the hotel's grand ballroom.

And if she was lucky, precisely two hours before the social hour, she'd take care of that itch that was threatening to consume her.

Wyatt spent most of the day between the convention center and the hotel, double-checking with Preston, Arthur and Joe at intervals to make sure all their bases were covered and nothing slipped through. When it was time to meet Fiona in her room, he couldn't deny the rapid beat of his heart or the fact that his jeans had become two times tighter than they'd been all day. Standing outside the room they'd shared the night before, he raised his hand to knock instead of running his keycard through the locking mechanism. He had yet to find another room, the concierge insisting all the rooms in the River Walk area had been overbooked and he'd be lucky to find anything until after the convention.

Drawing in a deep breath, he knocked, telling himself he'd be in and out as soon as she imparted the information he'd need to mingle at the party effectively.

Less than a second passed and the door swung open.

His lips quirked. She must have been waiting on the other side. It was nice to know she had been as anxious as he had been for the agreed upon hour to arrive. She stood in the doorway, naked, her long red hair hanging down over one of her shoulders, barely covering the tip of one breast.

All good intentions of remaining hands off flew out the window.

She grabbed his hand, yanked him through the doorway and shut it behind him.

He swallowed hard, his fingers tightening around hers to keep him from reaching out to capture one of her perfectly formed breasts.

Focus on the eyes.

"Uh, did I catch you at a bad time?" he asked, his gaze slipping from her eyes down to her smiling lips and lower to those smooth mounds jutting out as perky as ever, the tips knotted into hard little buds, tempting him to perdition. *Oh boy.*

"You and I both know this is as good a time as any." She reached out, grabbed his T-shirt and pulled it up over his head, tossing it over the back of a chair. "We have exactly one hour before I have to be in the ballroom directing the preparations." Her fingers made quick work of the button on his jeans, pushing it through and then sliding the zipper down.

His cock sprang free, hard, thick and throbbing. Wyatt groaned. "I told you, I'm no good for you."

"Let me be the judge of that." She stared down at his manhood. "Lose the boots," she commanded, as she cupped her breasts and squeezed the tips. "I don't know how long I can wait."

Surrendering to her demands, he toed off his cowboy boots and shucked his jeans in record time. "This changes nothing." He scooped her up into his arms and strode across the room to the bed, vaguely noting the rollaway had been removed. Nothing got in the way of the two of them and the mattress they'd be testing for endurance.

He tossed her in the middle and climbed in beside her, taking one of those sexy nipples into his mouth. Sucking hard on it, he released it and kissed his way across to the other. "Shouldn't we be checking on something?"

"Umm, yeah. On how wet you make me." Fiona ran her fingers down her torso to the juncture of her thighs, parting her folds for him.

"Got it." He took over, pushing her fingers aside. Her pussy was wet with thick, musky juices. Wyatt slipped two fingers into her channel, swirling around to drench them before sliding up to stroke her clit.

Fiona arched her back off the bed. "Oh yes. That's it. That's the spot." Her heels dug into the mattress and her bottom lifted.

Her apparent satisfaction spurred his desire. When he sat up, she touched his side. "I want to taste you," she said, her hand finding and gripping his dick, tugging him toward her. "Let me." Angling him toward her, she nudged his knees, urging him to straddle her head and lower himself until she could take his straining cock into the warmth and wetness of her mouth.

By all that was paradise, he couldn't think past the way she made him feel with her lips wrapped around him, the suction of her mouth pulling him deeper. Fiona gripped his ass and pulled him down until his cock bumped against the back of her throat.

He groaned and rose. Again, her fingers dug into his butt and she brought him back to her, fully encasing him with her mouth. He almost shot his wad right then.

Several deep breaths and a will of iron got him under control and he moved in and out, settling into a smooth, easy rhythm he could handle while he bent to the task of bringing her to the same heights of ecstasy.

Parting her folds with his fingers, he stroked his tongue across the tip of her clit.

Her ass rose from the bed and she moaned around his cock.

Wyatt flicked her clit again and then ran his tongue in a long, thick sweep that ended at her entrance where he tasted the musky cream of her desire. He dug his tongue into her channel, while he fingered the tight little hole of her anus.

Her knees came up to squeeze around his ears and her teeth scraped his dick.

If he wasn't careful, he'd come in her mouth. She had him so hot he could easily forget himself.

Focusing on her, he swiped and swirled his tongue along the swollen strip of flesh until she cried out, the noise muffled by his dick in her mouth.

She drew him deep into her mouth, her fingernails digging into his buttocks, holding him deep inside her.

Wyatt tensed, hovering on the edge, his body straining for release. Seconds before he lost it, he pulled free of her lips and turned around in the bed, settling between her legs. "Protection," he gritted out.

She held up a foil package in triumph, then tore it with her teeth and rolled the condom over his engorged cock, her fingers lingering at the base, rolling his balls between her digits.

The urgency of his desire won out and he thrust into her, pumping in and out so hard and fast the friction made their connection burn.

She rose up to meet him, their bodies slamming together in a hot and powerful union. When he could hold back no longer, he rose up on his knees, shoved a pillow beneath her hips, gathered her bottom in his grip and rammed into her one last time, burying his dick as deep as it would go. He held her there as he shot over the edge, his cock throbbing against the walls of her channel. At that moment, his entire world consisted of him and her and the bed they lay on. There was nowhere else he'd rather be.

Fiona wrapped her legs around his waist, digging her heels into his ass. She fondled her breasts, tweaking the nipples, her head thrashing side to side as her body shook with her own release.

When he finally came back down to earth, Wyatt pulled the pillow out from beneath her. Without breaking their connection, he lay on his side, rolling her over to face him. "I didn't come here to fuck you."

She smiled and kissed his chin. "But aren't you glad you did?"

He closed his eyes. "You know I am." He brushed a strand of hair away from her face. "I could easily become addicted to you."

"And that's a crime?" Fiona cupped his cheek. "I'm tough. I can handle more than you think."

He shook his head. "I was trained to kill and I almost killed you this morning."

"But you didn't." She smoothed a thumb across his mouth and leaned close to capture his lip between her teeth. Her breath was clean and minty and made him want to...

He crushed her mouth with his, his tongue pushing past her teeth to caress hers in a long sensuous glide. When he broke off, he pressed his forehead to hers. "My life is too complicated. I'm messed up. I'm only good for fighting. I will probably be leaving the country as soon as this assignment is over."

"I'll take what I can get." Fiona captured his hand on her face and pressed a kiss into his palm. "I stay very busy with my business. I'm not clingy and I'm not prone to wandering."

"You deserve a man who will treat you like a queen and will be home every night to do this."

"I don't want to be treated like a queen. I work for a living, and I like it that way. And if I can do this every so often...well...it's enough." She slipped his hand down to her left breast. "I want a man who treats a woman not like a queen, but like a woman. A man who captures my heart, who works hard and plays hard."

"Trust me, Fiona." He shook his head. "I'm not the one for you."

She gave him half a smile. "Because you don't find me absorbingly intelligent or attractive?"

Wyatt chuckled. "Actually, the opposite. I find you very intelligent and totally attractive. That's the problem."

"Sorry, I'm not seeing the problem." She kissed his chin and worked her way up to his lips. "Nope. Not seeing it."

He returned the kiss, cupping the back of her head, his fingers tangling in her crazy red curls. How did she manage to look so trim and sophisticated as she had appeared earlier in her gray suit, every hair in place? Wyatt liked her better like this. Wild, uncontrolled and sexy as hell. "You are absolutely beautiful. But I can't stay. When this gig is up, I'm gone." He kissed her one last time, hard and final. Then he rolled out of the bed, slapped her fanny and said, "You don't have much time before you need to be in the ballroom. Since I don't have to be there as early, you can have the bathroom first." He peeled off the condom and dropped it into the waste basket by the desk.

Fiona sat up and slid to her feet. "My door's always open to you. Should you change your mind." With a flip of her hair over her shoulder, she walked to the bathroom, the sway of her hips more emphasized than usual.

His cock responded, jerking to attention.

When she looked back and winked, he dove for the door and hustled her into the shower, climbing in behind her. "You're testing me, aren't you?" he said, nibbling the back of her neck.

"I'm a very determined woman." She tilted her head to the side, allowing him to kiss his way down her throat. "I get what I want."

"Umm. I don't doubt that." He cupped her breasts and bent to capture one, licking the water off the tip before sucking it into his mouth. Then he lifted her, wrapping her legs around his waist, backing her into the tile wall of the shower.

"And I want you." She wiggled her way down until her pussy hovered over his cock.

Damn, she had a way of keeping him hard. Wyatt drove into her, again and again, amazed at how quickly he'd recovered from their last round. How quickly he rose to the peak and would have exploded inside her, but he resisted, pulling free at the last moment. His cock was so hard he could drive nails into the wall with it.

Fiona gasped. "Why'd you stop?"

He shook his head and said through clenched teeth, "As crazy as you make me, we don't have protection."

"Let me down," she insisted.

Wyatt eased her to her feet and gripped his member, rubbing his hands along the length to finish what they'd started.

She grabbed the bar of soap and created a thick lather in her hands, then pushed his hands out of the way and wrapped hers around him. Within seconds of pumping up and down his shaft, she had him back where he'd left off inside her. One more jerk of her wrists sent him flying over the edge, shooting his wad over her hands.

Fiona glanced up and smiled and handed him the bar of soap. "Your turn."

He lathered up and ran his hands over her shoulders and arms, cupping her breasts in his big hands. They were perfect.

Fiona closed her eyes, letting her head tip back in the spray of the showerhead.

Wyatt trailed soap down her belly and wove his fingers through the tuft of curls covering her sex. Parting her folds, he flicked the nubbin hidden between.

Her breath hitched and she covered his hand with hers, urging him to continue. "Oh yeah. That's the spot."

Flicking again, he smiled at the way her face and body tensed. She responded to him so readily. With his other hand, he dug thumb into her pussy, and a single digit into her anus, taking up the rhythm of the strokes he applied to her clit.

Before long, she was hanging onto his arms, breathing hard, her body tense. "Holy hell," she said as she dug her fingernails into his muscles. "I can't...take...much...awwww." She flung back her head and rode his fingers, her hips thrusting against him, her face strained, her eyes squeezed shut.

He continued until she touched his hand. "Please. I can't take more. It's too much."

Wyatt slid his hands over her bottom and pressed her body against his, his cock sandwiched between them. "You are an incredible woman. Did you know that?"

Fiona laughed shakily, pushing her hair back from her face and letting the water run through it.

Her breasts bobbed and Wyatt seized their temptation, tweaking them briefly before squirting shampoo into his hands. "Much as I want to do this all again. I know you have to get done. Turn around."

She obeyed. Her pale back and bottom were every bit as sexy as her front. Ready to tell the world to screw itself, Wyatt squelched his continued desire for this amazing woman and applied the shampoo to her long red hair, working it through the tresses to her scalp.

"I've never had a man wash my hair before." She moaned softly. "Umm. I could get used to it."

He bit his tongue to keep from telling her he'd do it for her any time she liked. Being with Fiona made him forget his troubles. All he had to do was fall asleep with her in his arms and they'd start all over again. He could never forgive himself if he hurt her because of his nightmares. Finishing, he turned her around and let her rinse the soap out of her hair. Knowing he should get out of the shower and let her finish on her own, he just couldn't. He followed through with conditioner. The water began to cool and they finally climbed out of the shower and spent a few precious minutes drying each other off, laughing in the process.

Wyatt had never felt more relaxed in any other woman's company and he was liking it far too much.

Then Fiona made the mistake of checking the clock on her cell phone and shrieked. "Crap, I have ten minutes to get to the ballroom."

"You look great just the way you are." Wyatt slapped her ass.

Fiona turned and touched his chest, her hand drifting down to his still hardened member. "You look pretty good yourself." Then her eyes widened. "Crap. I didn't even think about it. Do you have a suit and tie? The event tonight is formal. You can't come in jeans and a T-shirt, and I really need you there. You didn't even bring a hanging bag or anything." She grabbed a brush and started yanking it through her hair. "There are stores in the River Center Mall if you need to be fitted quickly. But that's cutting it way too close. Does Joe have a suit you could use?"

Pushing back his laughter, he captured her hand to keep it from flapping. "I think I can come up with something."

She let out a steadying breath. "Oh good. Then go!" With a gentle shove, she guided him toward the bathroom door. "I'll never get ready on time if you stay in here. Damn, I haven't even dried my hair."

Wyatt laughed out loud as she closed the door in his face.

Fiona met Maddie in the ballroom an hour before the event was due to begin. She'd barely had time to dry and pin her hair up and thank goodness she'd had her dress dry cleaned and hanging in her closet. After she and Maddie attended to the last minute details with the hotel staff, Preston's security detail and Joe's dogs, Fiona smoothed imaginary wrinkles out of her dress and waited at the entrance to the ballroom, greeting the guests one at a time as they filed in.

She'd practiced greetings in eight different languages and used those on the diplomats as she checked them off her list. Twenty minutes into the social hour she still hadn't seen Wyatt and had begun to think he hadn't had any luck locating the appropriate attire for the formal event. Damn, she wished she'd thought of it earlier.

Maddie leaned toward her. "Columbia and Venezuela are getting a little too close."

Fiona glanced across the room.

The Columbian and the Venezuelan delegates were closing in on each other.

"Want me to run interference?" Maddie asked.

"No, I've got this." Fiona hurried across the room to avert confrontation, hooking the Columbian's arm and steering him away from the Venezuelan and toward the beautifully prepared hors d'oeuvres the hotel staff had prepared. When she'd introduced him to a woman from Argentina, she excused herself and glanced up as another guest entered the ballroom door. At that moment, the crowd separated long enough for her to catch a glimpse of the latest attendee.

A tall man dressed in a sharply tailored military uniform stepped into the room. Rows and rows of ribbons with shiny metals dangling off them adorned his chest. As he entered the ballroom, every female gaze shifted toward him.

His hair cut short, his chin cleanly shaven, he stood straight, his broad shoulders held back, his chest prominent and his mouth set in a straight line. Everything about him exuded power and dignity.

Fiona's heart did a double beat when she realized it was Wyatt.

"Wow," she said.

"Perdón, senorita?" The Mexican delegate leaned toward her.

"Pardon me." Fiona left the man standing there without another word and sifted through the throng toward the entrance.

When his gaze captured hers, his eyes widened ever so slightly and appreciatively, sweeping over her length.

She was glad she'd found the simple black gown on sale at one of San Antonio's most exclusive formal wear shops. With its V neckline and rhinestone straps it had been a particularly fabulous find. And based on the desire flaring in Wyatt's eyes, it was a keeper.

Feeling like a schoolgirl on her first date, she held out her hand. "You look amazing."

"You don't look so bad yourself." Without seeming to bend, he leaned toward her and whispered, "Only I prefer you naked."

Her cheeks warmed. "Nice to see you found something to wear."

"This old thing?" He winked and raised her hand to his lips, pressed a kiss to her palm and curled her fingers around it. He glanced around the room. "Everyone seems fairly civil at the moment."

"So far so good."

"In that case, would you care to dance?"

"Are you allowed to in uniform?" she asked.

He smiled and drew her hand through the crook of his arm. "Only with a beautiful woman."

She turned and let him lead her to the dance floor. The string quartet she'd hired was set up on a raised platform in the corner. Fortunately the sick person was well enough and had made it to the hotel. They'd just started into beautiful, flowing waltz. Fiona hesitated as they neared the open polished wood of the dance floor. No one else was dancing. "Are you sure?" She turned to face him. "Have you ever waltzed?"

He smiled down at her with that sexy, confident smile. "You know I can hold my own on the dance floor, darlin'."

Fiona chewed on her bottom lip. "Clubbing is different than dancing at a black tie affair."

He placed his hand on her naked back and guided her onto the floor, holding her other hand in his. "I think I can manage."

Without another word, he swept her up into the rhythm of the waltz, his steps perfect, his hand firm on her body, guiding her with each turn. She could have been a princess at a royal ball and Wyatt the prince, smiling down at her. Fiona had to stop herself from saying wow again. The man had so much charm, confidence and sex appeal, he melted her knees with just a look.

And in uniform...just wow.

As the song came to an end, Fiona sighed, disappointed. In Wyatt's arms, she could forget everything else. "Where did you learn to dance like that?"

"My mother taught me how to waltz when I was a little boy. And like I said, I got a lot of practice at the country western honky-tonk some of us hung out at outside Fort Bragg during training."

"Well, congratulate your mother for me. You did her proud."

He grinned. "She is a remarkable woman."

Fiona's brows rose. "What about your father?"

"That old coot is still alive and kickin' as well. He's ornery enough to outlive me by a long shot."

"I bet there's a lot of him in you."

Wyatt nodded. "Too much at times. If we spend time together, we end up buttin' heads." A smile softened his words. "But he's a good man beneath the gruffness."

Fiona could imagine an older version of Wyatt and wondered what it would be like to grow old with him? Would he be content to sit on a porch and rock through his retirement? Or would he still be charging headfirst into one adventure after another? Fiona suspected the latter and realized she'd prefer the same. Too bad this impressive soldier was so dead set on keeping their relationship casual and ending it upon the conclusion of this event.

With a sigh, Fiona waved toward the table laden with every kind of fancy finger food imaginable. "Hungry?"

His hand tightened around her waist. "Not for food."

"There's nothing I'd like more than to slip out of here and out of my dress and heels and make love to you, but my presence is required."

Wyatt glanced around the room and back to her. "Is there a coat closet or an office we could duck into? I'm betting you aren't wearing underwear beneath that dress."

She let her lips curl up slightly on the corner. "You'll just have to keep guessing until all the guests leave the party, now, won't you?"

Wyatt growled low in his chest. "Want me to clear them out of here?"

Her eyes widened. "No, I do not. Besides, you wouldn't want to wrinkle that pretty uniform."

"Pretty?" He stood even taller, if that was at all possible. "I'll have you know, Special Forces soldiers aren't pretty. It's not regulation."

Fiona laughed. "Okay, then how about sexy uniform?"

He relaxed beside her and smiled. "That's better. Can't lose my macho appeal with a single word."

Fiona snorted softly. "As if you could lose an ounce of macho. You're practically bursting at the seams with swagger."

"How long is this going on?"

Fiona smiled. "It'll all be over by ten."

"Good. I don't know if I can stand wearing this tie that long."

"If I can stand in these heels, you can wear a tie."

"I'd rather you and I were naked."

"I thought you weren't anxious to continue our relationship?"

"You and I both know that after this event is over, I'm out of here. But while I'm here..." He tugged at his tie. "Damn, woman, you're making this hard on me."

Her smile tilted upward. "That's the idea."

One of the attendees called out to Fiona.

She sighed. "That's my cue."

"Go. I want to have a look around the building and parking garage. I'll be back as soon as I can."

She reluctantly left Wyatt to attend to the guests, making introductions to the visiting delegates and government officials. After a while her lips hurt from smiling, and if she had to shake one more gorilla hand bent on crushing her bones... Fiona counted the minutes until she could strip out of her dress and get naked with Wyatt again. By thirty minutes until ten o'clock, the party was in full swing and still she'd seen no sign of Wyatt.

Chapter Nine

Wyatt checked with every guard at every entrance to the hotel, saving the front entrance and the parking lot in the basement for last. As he stepped out the lobby door, he spied Joe and Bacchus surrounded by two very elegant beauties dressed to the hilt in low-slung gowns displaying more flesh than the material they were made of covered.

Joe, dressed in tailored slacks, a black button-down shirt and black necktie, with his short hair and blue eyes, probably appealed to the opposite sex. Add the dog he was obviously attached to and he was a veritable chick magnet.

When Wyatt appeared at Joe's side, the ladies' attention shifted to him and the shiny medals on his chest. For a moment he wished he still wore the jeans and T-shirt he'd had on most of the day. These women did not interest him in the least. Normally, he'd flirt and maybe even take a number and one of or both of them to bed.

But his mind was back in the ballroom with a feisty redhead and he couldn't wait to get back and maybe catch another dance with her. She moved like an angel on wings. Only she was as sexy as the devil.

"Are you here for the convention?" The tall blonde asked while her shorter, brunette friend smiled shyly at him.

"Yes, ma'am."

"Well, then, I'm glad I went to the trouble to come to this little party." The blonde walked her fingers up his chest to the shiny medals pinned to his jacket. "And what are all these pretty coins for?"

He grabbed her hand before she could put fingerprints all over the shiny medal. "Ma'am, I'm on duty." Wyatt set her aside, gently but firmly.

"My apologies. My name is Brigitte." The woman held out her hand as if to shake his.

Reluctantly he took hers and she deposited a keycard in his palm, leaned close and whispered, "Room two-eleven."

"Ma'am, you don't want to lose this." He handed it back to her and stepped back.

When the blonde frowned and opened her mouth to say something, Joe loosened his grip on Bacchus's lead and the dog pressed his nose to the woman's crotch.

She squealed and jumped back. "Get that filthy creature away from me!"

"Sorry, ma'am. Bacchus, like some people, forgets his manners on occasion."

Her cheeks reddened and she sputtered. "Well, I never."

"Yes, ma'am." Joe smiled. "I'm sure you never."

The woman pulled herself up to her full height. "Come on, Meredith."

The brunette giggled. "I seem to have dropped my lipstick tube. I'll be with you in a minute, Brigitte."

When Brigitte had gone into the hotel, Meredith smiled. "Bacchus is a rascal." She bent to scratch the dog's ears. "Or is it his master who's the rascal?" She glanced up, her smile remaining firm, her brows raised in question.

Joe shrugged. "Can't say. I don't speak dog."

Meredith winked. "I think you understand Bacchus better than you let on." She held out her hand. He took it, tentatively. "Nice to meet you."

Meredith grinned up at Wyatt and followed the blonde into the hotel.

Joe bent to pat Bacchus head. "He's a better judge of character than most people."

Wyatt laughed. "You can say that again." He glanced at the brunette as she disappeared into the lobby. "You could have had her number by just asking."

His friend shook his head. "Not sure I'm ready."

Wyatt understood exactly what Joe was saying. "Do you think we'll ever be ready again?"

Joe scrubbed a hand over his jaw. "I hope so. That one caught my interest enough to think about it. I suppose that's heading in the right direction."

An image of Fiona standing naked in the shower flashed in Wyatt's mind and he pushed it firmly back. "How's it going out here?"

"So far so good. Only had to turn away one drunk and one salesman."

Wyatt glanced around. "I thought Preston was going to man the front with you."

"He only stuck around for the first hour. I haven't seen him since. Said something about checking out the east entrance."

"I was just there and didn't see him."

Joe touched his radio. "Try him on the box?"

Wyatt nodded. "Twice. No answer."

Tapping the side of his handheld radio, Joe shook his head. "That's the one thing we could count on in the army, good radios."

"These aren't bad. I tested them thoroughly earlier today, before Fiona issued them to us. They were working fine then and they have fresh batteries."

"Guess you'll have to find him without technology." Joe jerked his head toward the door. "How's it going inside?"

"So far no major incidents."

"I caught a glimpse of Fiona." Joe's mouth quirked at the corners. "Just tell me you're not interested and I'll be all over her like a dog on a bone."

Wyatt's jaw tightened and his eyes narrowed in a glare. "I thought you weren't ready for a relationship?"

Joe raised his hands. "Just sayin'. She's a looker, that one."

Wyatt knew. She looked good in her evening gown with her hair piled high on her head. Fiona looked even better naked, wet and panting in the middle of hot and heavy sex.

His cock twitched and he had to remind himself not to get too stirred up while in uniform. His trousers were tailor-made with no pleats to allow for sudden expansion of parts farther south.

"Would love to be a fly on the wall in there. I hear there are several dignitaries not too proud to pick a fight."

"You want to take a turn around the ballroom?" Wyatt asked, knowing the answer before he asked the question. Joe had a distinct aversion to formal events. The black slacks, shirt and tie were his only concessions to being strapped into a monkey suit for hours.

"Hell no. That kind of stuff gives me the willies." Joe nodded toward Wyatt. "You trying to impress Fiona with that chest full of medals?"

Heat rose up Wyatt's neck. "Not really. It was the closest thing I had to a tuxedo. And I only wear it once a year. Didn't see spending good money on tuxedo rental."

Joe shivered. "Can't see how you wear it. Too confining for me. Reminds me of wearing flack vests in Fallujah. Couldn't breathe in all that equipment, much less maneuver fast enough to keep from being shot."

They'd been together in the fight to capture Fallujah, taking one building at a time. The tension had been palpable and they'd all been on their toes. This situation didn't call for an enemy around every corner, but it had its moments of tension. Though nothing like what they'd experienced in Iraq or Afghanistan. And nothing at all like what he'd endured in Somalia. Yeah, it was good to be back in the States for a while.

Glancing around once more at the relative calm of the activities at the entrance, Wyatt nodded. "I'm going to find Preston, then I'm headed back into the ballroom."

"Better you than me and Bacchus. Although Bacchus likes the music." Joe's lips twisted. "When someone leaves the door open long enough, his tail starts twitching to the beat."

As if on cue, a guest passed through the entrance and paused. The music from the ballroom drifted out to where they stood and Bacchus's tail swished back and forth in rhythm.

A brief smile slipped across Wyatt's face. He was glad his buddy Joe had Bacchus and his dog training business. Without it, he'd have fallen victim to PTSD, alcohol and possibly drug addiction.

For once, Wyatt was really happy to be in San Antonio instead of back in Somalia. And he realized much of his relief was due to his focus on Fiona. He was also glad that the danger here seemed limited to cat fights between delegates, versus hard to find and uproot Somali militants and Al-Qaeda terrorists.

Ducking back through the front door, he headed for the elevator, stepped in and punched the down button for the parking garage, the last place he planned to check anyway. Perhaps Preston was making his rounds and had ended up there.

When Wyatt stepped out of the elevator into the echoing, concrete walls of the parking garage, he was struck first by the lack of a guard on the elevator. His instincts perked and he loosened the button on his jacket to make it easier for him to reach for the gun nestled in the shoulder holster beneath.

There were two sub-levels to the parking garage. As he moved through the bays filled with vehicles, he didn't spot even one guest. But something strange caught his attention on one of the concrete support pillars in a dark corner of the garage. A flashing red light blinked at him. As he neared it, he noted the creamy white clay-like substance, wrapped in black electrical tape, a mechanical box settled in the middle with wires poking out of it.

Wyatt's gut clenched. He knew exactly what it was, having worked with it on many operations in Iraq, Afghanistan and Somalia.

C-4 explosives equipped to be remotely detonated.

Not knowing how many of the devices there could be in the building or when whoever had set them planned to detonate, he did the only thing he could think of, and yanked the wires out of the detonator, disabling the unit.

He got on his radio. "Joe, we have a problem."

"Tell me," Joe responded.

"C-4 in the parking garage, wired for remote detonation. I think Preston set them."

"Fuck. I'll start the evacuation up here. You better get out while you can."

"Make it quiet. If Preston is still down here, he has a detonator. I don't want him alerted that we're on to him." Wyatt's jaw hardened. Why hadn't Preston set off the explosions? The man had issues. Perhaps he could be talked out of destroying the hotel and the people in it. "I'm going to see if I can stop this."

"Wyatt, this world doesn't need another hero."

"Just get them all out. And make sure Fiona is one of those evacuated, will ya?"

"Got it. Once the evacuation is underway, I'll bring Bacchus down. He's trained to sniff out C-4."

"Deal."

His heart pounding against his ribs, Wyatt raced through the garage, spotting two more of the lumps of clay-like charges, pulling the detonators from those as well. He couldn't be sure he had them all and in the meantime, he had to get the people out of the building.

A car had just pulled into a parking space and the driver got out, spotting Wyatt coming toward him, he asked, "Is the hotel for the International Trade Convention social?"

Wyatt hurried up to the driver. When he was close enough to whisper, he told him, "Get out of the garage. Now."

"But we just got here," the man replied. "Is something wrong?"

Wyatt snorted. He didn't have time to stop and explain. "There are bombs planted all over this garage. If you want to live, get your date and get the hell out, quietly. The man responsible might still be down here."

The woman in the passenger seat cried out, jerked the door open and got to her feet.

The man grabbed the woman's hand and hustled her back out the ramp to the exit, hurrying her along in her high heels.

After disarming the charges he could find, Wyatt circled around the ramp heading into the bottom level of the parking garage. At first it appeared empty.

When he stepped out into the open, a shot rang out, nicking his arm. Wyatt dove behind a vehicle as another bang echoed against the walls.

"You can't stop this," a voice called out, one Wyatt recognized as Preston.

"Preston, whatever your issues are, we can get you help." Wyatt moved to the opposite end of the vehicle and eased around it.

"You have no idea what you're talking about."

Wyatt dropped to his chest and peered beneath the chassis of the Cadillac he was using for cover. He spotted Preston's legs moving toward the stairwell. "Try me, Preston. I'm listening."

"It's too late. I have to set these off before they evacuate."

"No, you don't. These people don't have to die. There are always solutions. Give yourself a chance."

"No. I'm done and all those people who've pretended to be our friends, the countries who say they're on our side and then kill us every chance they get, tonight, they'll know."

"What will they know, Preston?" Wyatt worked his way around one car, then another.

"The world will know that they all lie. We try to help them and they kill us. They killed every one of the men in my unit. And we were fucking trying to help them."

"Preston, I've been there," Wyatt called out softly. "I've seen my friends die in a battle we seem destined to lose. If we don't try, if we don't keep fighting for right, they win."

"That's just it. They've already won. Our government is too stupid to figure it out, and they want to keep giving the enemy money, keep educating them and building their fucking buildings for them. It's got to stop."

"This isn't the way to do it, Preston. Killing innocent people isn't the way to stop them."

"Maybe it'll make our enemies think before coming to our country and pretending they're on our side. I'm tired of diplomacy. It doesn't work."

While Preston had been talking, Wyatt worked his way around the ends of half a dozen cars. He could see Preston pushing more C-4 into place with the detonator already strapped to it.

Wyatt started to stand. A loud bang exploded close by and a bullet pinged off the car beside him.

"Get back, Magnus. I don't have a beef with you. If you want to live, get out now." He fired at him again and ran for the staircase.

Wyatt raced after him, but didn't reach him before the door closed and a bullet fired into the lock disabled it. He couldn't follow Preston using that route, so he ran to the elevator, and punched the up arrow, speaking into his handheld radio. "Joe."

"Wyatt, where are you?"

The door opened and he stepped in. "Coming up from the garage. It *is* Preston. He's got some bone to pick with foreign countries and has set C-4 charges in the parking garage. He got away from me and is headed up. I don't know where. And he's also armed and has already fired at me several times."

"Damn. I should have known he was a loose cannon when Bacchus growled at him. Look, they're taking all the delegates from the ballroom out into the side alley," Joe informed him. "I'm at the front entrance, monitoring progress."

"Do you have a visual on Fiona and Maddie?"

"I saw Maddie out front, but not Fiona." Joe cut out for a moment. "Sorry, someone bumped into me. Place is crazy. But I'll let you know when I see them."

"Thanks, man."

"Don't worry, Magnus, I'll keep an eye out for your girl."

"Gotta go. I'm on my way up to the lobby." Wyatt burst through the door into the richly carpeted reception area on the lobby level. Women dressed in ball gowns and men in tuxedos or black suits hurried toward the exit. Some of the hotel guests wore bathrobes and bedroom slippers as if they'd just gone to bed when the evacuation had begun.

Hotel staff apologized for the inconvenience as they assured the guests they'd get to the bottom of the problem as soon as possible, while they ushered them out the door.

A child whimpered, a man called out to his wife and everyone was talking at once. But all in all it was more of a controlled chaos with the mass of people moving steadily outside.

They just weren't moving fast enough. If Preston set off the charges...

Wyatt exited through the side door, searching the crowd of faces for Fiona, the darkness and people standing around hampering his efforts.

His radio chirped and he held it to his mouth. "Find her?" he barked.

"No. She's not out the front of the building, nor is she answering her radio. I'm headed around the side."

"Fuck. I'm here on the side of the building. She's not here either."

Sirens sounded in the distance, headed their way.

Wyatt pushed his way back to the door. "I'm going back in."

"The staff is blocking the exits, waiting for the fire department to arrive. They're only allowing people out. No one is going in."

"Bullshit." When Wyatt reached the exit door he'd come out of, he tried the handle. It was locked.

Damn. He was turning toward the front of the building when the door opened and the man he recognized as the Brazilian delegate pushed through with a beautiful woman clinging to his arm, her makeup smeared from tears. She spoke in rapid Portuguese and a fresh round of tears erupted.

Wyatt dove for the door before it swung shut and reentered the hotel.

"Sir, no one is allowed back inside."

"It's okay, I'm head of the security staff," Wyatt said.

"We were under strict instructions to get everyone out. The bomb squad is on its way. You can't go inside."

The man blocked Wyatt's path.

His heartbeat hammering in his chest, every combat instinct sprang to life. Wyatt's eyes narrowed and he had to remind himself the staff member was not his enemy. "Move out of my way, or I'll move you out of my way. And trust me, you won't like the way I move you."

Something in the steely tone of his voice got through to the man because he stepped to the side. "You're on your own, buddy. I'm not taking responsibility for your life if this building explodes." The man pushed past him and exited through the door he'd been guarding.

Wyatt raced for the ballroom.

The room was empty, the picked-over tables of food standing as a reminder of the festivities that only a few minutes before had been underway. No one had stayed.

If she wasn't out front or at the side entrance, where could Fiona have gone?

Surely she hadn't tried to go up to their rooms or to one of the floors to help someone else get out of the hotel?

Someone had turned off the elevators. Wyatt headed for the stairwell and ran up the flights of stairs stopping at every floor to check the hallways. "Fiona!" he yelled. No one stirred on the first or second floors. When he reached the third floor, he hurried down the hallway to the room he'd shared with Fiona and swiped his key through the card reader.

She wasn't in the bedroom or bathroom touching up her makeup. Nor was she in the hallway or at either entrance to the entire building. How had he missed her?

His pulse pounding, Wyatt ran back down to the lobby level and stood for a moment in the empty space. Even the hotel staff had left. The faint sound of emergency vehicles heralded the arrival of the fire department and police.

So far he didn't smell any smoke and nothing had exploded. He didn't like that the hotel guests had all been herded out into the open where any fool could take a shot at them. Including Preston. Hopefully, with police and firemen surrounding the area, nothing would happen to the guests. He prayed they all got out safely, Fiona with them. He'd only known her for a little more than twenty-four hours. From pulling her out of the river to making love to her twice to waltzing with her in his mess dress uniform, he'd packed a lot of getting to know her into the short time they'd been together. Damned if he didn't like her drive, determination and gumption. Yeah, he liked her a lot. Too much to walk away, which would be the smartest thing to do for both him and her.

Maybe he'd consider leaving her, once he found her and was certain she was safely outside the building.

Where could she be? Wyatt closed his eyes for a moment and used a technique he'd used to find Al-Qaeda militants, by thinking like they'd think.

What would Fiona do? How would she think? As organized as she was, she'd have counted heads of her guests to ensure all had made it out safely. Then she would have checked for all her security personnel. The woman was almost obsessive about tying up all the loose strings. She wouldn't rest until she had all her little chicks accounted for. In that case, she might be looking for him while he was looking for her.

He'd told her all the places he'd go to inspect. Logic dictated she'd look for him in those places, most of which he'd already covered since coming up from the garage. Could she have gone down while he'd been racing up? Damn. She'd be heading straight into the blast zone.

His eyes popped open and he ran for the closest staircase leading into the parking garage. When he reached first level, he shoved open the door and burst into the coolness.

A scream ripped through the air. Wyatt swung toward the sound, his gun drawn. That's when he saw her.

Preston had Fiona, his arm around her neck, dragging her backward toward a van. "Stay back, Magnus, or I'll hurt her."

"Let her go, Preston. She's not the problem."

"Maybe not, but she's my ticket out of here."

"Put down the gun, Preston," Fiona urged, her voice tight, constrained by the arm choking off the air to her vocal chords.

"No way. If I put it down, your boyfriend will shoot me."

Fiona's gaze met Wyatt's. "Put your gun down, Wyatt," she said. "Please."

Wyatt hesitated. Preston had already shot at him. The man was on the edge and could easily blow a gasket. "I'm going to put my weapon down, Preston. Don't shoot me and, be smart and don't hurt the lady. She's done nothing to hurt you or your buddies who died in the war."

"I don't want to hurt her, but I will if you do anything stupid." Preston nodded. "Drop it and kick it toward me."

Wyatt eased his arm down ever so slightly. Already Preston's gun dipped and his arm seemed to loosen.

Fiona jabbed her elbow into Preston's gut, slammed her high heel into his instep and ducked.

Wyatt yanked his weapon up and fired off a round at the same time as Preston.

Preston's shot went wide, hitting the concrete wall behind Wyatt.

Wyatt's shot flew true, crashing into Preston's chest, knocking him backward onto his ass. Because Fiona had been leaning against him, when he fell, she fell with him. She landed hard, rolled to the side, snatched up Preston's gun and turned before Wyatt could reach her.

She didn't need it. Preston was dead, but he was very much a threat to them and everyone else in the building. The remote detonator device was still clutched in his hand, though the man lay with his eyes open, staring vacantly at the ceiling.

Wyatt eased the device from the man's hand and laid it on the ground, gently, afraid if he left it in Preston's hand, he might have a dying man's muscle spasm and set off the explosives Wyatt hadn't found.

When he rose, Fiona flung herself into his arms, nearly knocking him off his feet. "Thank God he didn't hurt you."

"Me?" Wyatt chuckled, loving the feel of her warm body against his and holding her like there would be no tomorrow. For the two of them, it had nearly been the truth.

In those few short minutes when Preston had held Fiona, threatening to kill her, all the doubts Wyatt had about a real relationship with a woman blew out of his mind and his thoughts had become crystal clear. He wanted the chance to get to know Fiona. Not just her incredible body, but the brave, slightly high-strung, incredibly smart and sassy woman who might not have lived to see the next day of her life had Preston succeeded in his plan to blow a hole in downtown San Antonio.

"I was so afraid for you," he whispered against her hair, holding her so close he could feel her breath against his neck.

"I thought Preston had killed you or left you wounded somewhere." She leaned back, tears trickling down her face. "You don't know how happy I was to see you show up alive."

"Ditto, sweetheart." He crushed her lips with his, drawing the kiss out as long as they both had breath. When he finally raised his head, he cupped her cheeks in his palms. "I can't seem to get enough of you."

"It goes both ways, babe." Her gaze traveled over him. "I'm so sorry your uniform got so messed up—Wyatt, you're bleeding!" She tried to open his jacket, but he stopped her.

"I'm okay. The bullet only nicked me."

"Yeah and you're still bleeding." She glanced down at Preston. "Is it true he was planning to blow up the building with everyone in it?"

Wyatt's arm slipped around her waist. "Yes."

Fiona glanced around the parking lot. "Are there charges positioned down here?"

"I got what I could find, but I'm not sure I got them all. We should get out of here, just in case." Wyatt gripped her arm and led her toward the stairs.

Fiona dug her feet in, bringing him to a stop. "Are we going to leave him here?"

"There's nothing we can do for him."

She stared down at the man who'd tried to kill her and a lot of other people. "He must have been very unhappy."

"I suspect PTSD." His gaze captured hers. "It happens to the best of soldiers."

She slipped an arm around Wyatt's waist. "And that's why you don't want to stay." Her words were a statement, not a question. "But you know, it doesn't have to be that way. You don't have to leave."

"I can't put you in harm's way. Especially if the harm is in me."

"But you can't run from it. Wouldn't you be better off working through your issues with someone who cares than going it alone?" She smiled. "Joe seems to have recovered nicely with his friend, Bacchus."

"Are you volunteering to be my pet dog?" Wyatt grinned. "Sorry. Although you can wield a pretty wicked puppy-dog stare, you're not a dog." Gripping her hips, he pulled her against the hardness of his cock, straining against the fabric of his trousers. "You're one hundred percent woman and what you did tonight was purely heroic."

Color flew like pink flags in her cheeks. "No more than you did. Come on. Let's get out of here. I have to get back to the guests before we have another international incident." She poked a finger in his chest. "But you're not off the hook, so don't go disappearing on me. And we're going to have the medical personnel look at that wound, whether you think you need it or not."

Using his good arm, Wyatt popped a salute. "Yes, ma'am."

Fiona sniffed and gave him a satisfied nod. "Let's go, mister."

A chuckle rose up his throat and escaped, echoing off the walls of the stairwell, all the way up to the ground floor.

Wyatt couldn't believe his good luck getting to Preston before he could blow up the building, and to Fiona before Preston could kill her. Today just wasn't their day to die.

Chapter Ten

Early the next morning, after answering hundreds of questions for the police and then helping to coordinate the relocation of all the guests to other hotels throughout the city of San Antonio, Fiona lay naked in the bed in her apartment, exhausted, but too wound up to fall to sleep.

"I asked my commander to put me in for a training assignment at Fort Sam Houston, at least for the next six months." Wyatt emerged from the bathroom, strutting across the carpet naked from his toes to his very short haircut.

"And?" Fiona leaned up, her eyes wide, her breath hitched, waiting for his response.

"He gave me three months."

She fell back against the pillows. "Is that all?"

With a nod, he dropped onto the sheets beside her and stretched his long body out, pulling hers against him, his cock nudging her sex. "If you'd known how hard I pushed him to get out of here, you'd understand why that was a big concession on his part."

"And now?" Fiona kissed his beard-stubbled chin. "You don't want to leave so soon?"

He bent to nuzzle the pulse beating at the base of her throat. "Not so much. I've barely had time to get to know San Antonio."

She swatted at his uninjured arm, happy that he'd been correct that the bullet wound had only been superficial. Although it had ruined his uniform jacket. "Only San Antonio?"

"Oh yeah. And one hot, little redhead with a wicked elbow jab." He cupped her chin and kissed her, urging her to part her teeth and let him slide in to caress her tongue with his.

Fiona was amazed that such a big, rough man could be so gentle. All hard angles and scars, he knew exactly what to say and where to touch her to make her body sing.

When he ended the kiss, his finger trailed down her arm until his palm caressed her hip. "Are you sure about this…you and me…all night?" He let go of a long breath. "What if my nightmares get violent? I don't want to hurt you."

Fiona leaned up on her elbow. "Positive. I'll take my chances, since the rewards outweigh the danger." She drew her finger down his chest. "And I know, deep down in that soldier's heart of yours, that you're a good man."

"I can't control my dreams."

"Then I'll help you. I'm a light sleeper anyway and if you get restless, I'll move."

"Promise me you will." His finger tightened on her hips. "I could never forgive myself if I hurt you."

She smiled down at him and ran her hand along his rough beard. "I won't let you hurt me, so stop worrying and start loving me."

"Yes, ma'am." He rolled her onto her back and came up over her. "How about I begin my attack here?" Dropping low, he captured one of her nipples between his teeth and nibbled gently before sucking it fully into his mouth.

Fiona's heart swelled and she arched up to offer him the full benefit of her breast. "Now you're talking."

He didn't stop there, working his lips and tongued over the other breast before skimming across her ribs and lower to the mound of curls covering her sex. Pausing there, he parted her folds with the tips of his rough fingers and blew a warm stream of air over her heated center.

Too impatient to wait for it, Fiona gripped his ears and urged him down.

He settled between her legs and thrust his tongue into her channel, swirling around before coming up to lay siege to her clit.

Fiona cried out and surrendered to his attack, digging her heels into the mattress and rising up to press her pussy into his mouth.

One finger, then two and finally three entered her channel, another poked at the tight entrance to her anus. With his tongue teasing the nubbin packed full of exquisitely throbbing nerves, she shot to the heavens, screaming out his name. "Wyatt!"

His relentless pursuit wore away her will to live in a world without him and she rode the passionate wave to the pulsing end.

When she thought it couldn't get any better, he climbed up her body, rolled on a condom and thrust his thickened shaft into her, sliding through her slick entrance until his balls bumped against her ass.

"Oh yes!" she shouted, not caring whether or not the neighbors could hear her.

The mattress bounced, the springs squeaked and the headboard rammed the wall more than once before they reached a shared climax to beat all climaxes and slowly drifted back to earth.

Without breaking their connection, he pulled her into his arms and held her.

Fiona trailed a finger across his chest, tweaking the hard brown nipples, loving how solid his chest felt beneath her fingertips. She tipped his chin down and brushed her lips across his.

"Umm. I could go for more of this." Capturing his cheeks in between her palms, she deepened the kiss, sliding her tongue along the length of his, her thigh climbing up over his. "Got another condom?"

"Hell yeah." He rolled on another in record time.

She pressed her pussy down over his shaft, stirring him back to full thickness.

Wyatt laughed, his chest rumbling beneath hers. "All this because of a perky pair of pink shorts." Then he flipped her onto her back and thrust deep into her.

Fiona wrapped her legs around his waist and dug her heels into his ass, urging him to fuck harder, faster and longer. Her breath caught and she held it as she shot over the top, her senses cascading around her in tingling electrical bursts.

Wyatt slammed home one last time and held steady, his jaw tight, his dick pulsing inside her. When he dropped back down to the mattress beside her, he flung an arm over his face. "That was fucking amazing."

"I thought so." With a smile on her face, she snuggled up to his side, draping her hand across his middle, feeling the rise and fall of his chest. Content to lie there in silence, she pressed her lips to his closest nipple, noting the steady rhythm of his breathing.

Wyatt had fallen asleep.

Well into the morning, Fiona lay awake, waiting for soldier's nightmares.

They never came. Wyatt slept through without twitching, calling out or trying to choke her. With daylight edging around the corners of the blinds, Fiona let herself drift into a half-dream, half-awake state, more determined than ever and confident that with a little care and a lot of love, she could help declare a victory in Wyatt's War.

About the Author

ELLE JAMES also writing as MYLA JACKSON is a *New York Times* and *USA Today* Bestselling author of books including cowboys, intrigues and paranormal adventures that keep her readers on the edges of their seats. With over eighty works in a variety of sub-genres and lengths she has published with Harlequin, Samhain, Ellora's Cave, Kensington, Cleis Press, and Avon. When she's not at her computer, she's traveling, snow skiing, boating, or riding her ATV, dreaming up new stories.

Learn more about Elle James at
www.ellejames.com

Or visit her alter ego Myla Jackson at
www.mylajackson.com

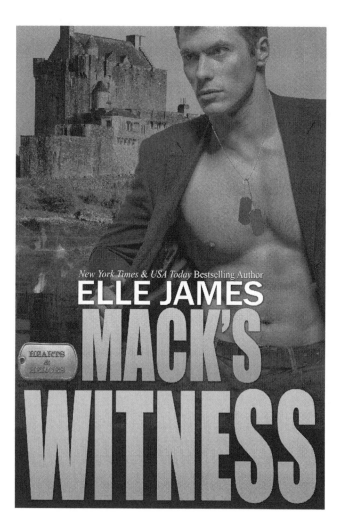

New York Times & USA Today Bestselling Author

ELLE JAMES

HEARTS & HEROES

MACK'S
WITNESS

MACK'S WITNESS

HEARTS & HEROES
BOOK 2

New York Times & *USA Today*
Bestselling Author

ELLE JAMES

Chapter One

"Captain Mack, sniper on the south corner of the building ahead."

"Keep him in your sights, Gunny." Mack Magnus led one squad of his men toward the village from the south, while two other squads flanked the village from the west.

His point man had the best eye for spotting trouble. If not for Gunnery Sergeant Roy Tyler's eagle eye, they'd have lost a lot more men in the thirteen months since they'd deployed to Camp Leatherneck in the Helmand Province of Afghanistan.

This particular night they were operating on intel indicating a Taliban stronghold had been established in the small village nestled in the rocky hills. They'd spent the better part of the day maneuvering into position to storm the village at night when the enemy slept. The problem usually arose when the Taliban surrounded themselves by innocent civilians—women and children. They knew the American soldiers would balk at destroying an entire village if innocents were involved.

Cowards. This particular faction had recently lit a teenaged girl on fire and thrown her out of a speeding vehicle in front of a checkpoint to make an example of people who sided with anyone but the Taliban.

Embedded news reporters had a field day with the horrific images. No one could get to the girl without taking on live fire. By the time they reached her, she'd been burned to death, her screams something he'd never forget.

The squad halted outside the walled village and waited for the other squads to maneuver into place. Then one-by-one they slipped over the wall and dropped down on the other side, moving through the village to the largest building at the center where a Taliban meeting was said to be taking place that night.

Earlier, they'd watched from the nearby hillsides as vehicles entered the walled village, some were trucks loaded down with men in turbans, carrying Russian-made AK47s. Others were vans or cars. For a small village where most inhabitants didn't own a motorized car or truck, it was a lot of movement.

Mack had waited until dark before giving the order to move out.

Now inside the compound, they moved toward the target. Gunny climbed to the top of the building where the sniper sat and dispatched the man before he could fire a single round. The man must have fallen asleep at his post. He'd never do that again.

As the squads moved on the main building at the center of the village, the first shot rang out.

"Let's rumble," Mack said into his mic as the other squads moved into position. With his night vision goggles in place, he took the lead, moving building to building, firing on Taliban sentries.

Gunny dropped down from the sniper's position and joined Mack and the rest of the squad rushing the building.

Mack reached for a concussion grenade clipped to his vest, pulled the pin, kicked in the door to the building and tossed the grenade inside.

He ducked to the side of the door and held his hands over his ears as did the others. The grenade went off with a muffled whomp. His feet vibrated beneath him and the wall he leaned on shook.

Then he moved into the building and stepped over the bodies of two men and gathered the guns they'd carried, handing them back to Gunny, who would quickly strip the bolts out of the weapons and slam the stock into the wall to break it against any future attempt at use against American forces.

The deeper he moved into the structure, the more he realized there were no other men but the original sentries.

"Got trouble on the south side of the village!" Someone shouted into his headset.

Sounds of rifle reports came to Mack through the thick walls. Mack pointed to the exit and shouted, "Go! Go! Go!"

As he emerged from the building, he nearly tripped over Lance Corporal Jenson lying on his side moaning, his hand clutching his thigh drenched in blood.

A bullet hit the building over Mack's right shoulder, dusting him in powder and pebbles from the stucco.

He dropped to his haunches and glanced up through his night vision goggles. On the top corner of the building down the street from where he crouched, he saw the green heat signature of a warm body and the bright flash of bullet rounds. Mack raised his rifle to his shoulder, held his breath and squeezed the trigger. The man on the roof tipped over and fell to the ground.

Mack shouted, "Gunny, stay here and help Jenson."

"Yes, sir." Gunny bent over the lance corporal, administering a quick field dressing and light tourniquet to slow the bleeding.

Mack moved through the maze of streets and walled yards, following the sound of rifle fire, hurrying to join the others.

As he rounded a corner, something dropped in front of him and rolled.

"Grenade!" he shouted and threw himself back around the corner, knocking into the rest of his squad.

A loud bang shook the earth.

"Sir." A slender hand shook his shoulder and a voice with a light Irish lilt said, "Sir, we've just landed at Dublin International Airport. Are ya all right?"

Mack blinked awake and sat up straighter, taking a moment to orient himself to his environment. "Dublin?"

"Yes, sir." The diminutive, older woman sitting beside him smiled. "You were having a wee bit of a bad dream."

Mack ran a hand down his face, wishing he'd had time to scrape the day's growth of beard off before heading straight for his brother's bachelor party. Hell, he'd like to have slept a day or two before the events. He'd pulled every string to fly out of Afghanistan a day earlier than the remainder of his unit re-deploying stateside.

"Are ya here on business or pleasure?" the woman asked as the plane taxied down the runway to the terminal.

He hadn't talked the entire trip, closing his eyes as soon as the plane took off from Frankfurt. He'd arrived at Ramstein Air Force Base and made a mad dash to the international airport at Frankfurt, Germany, to catch his flight to Ireland. Exhausted and in need of rest, he'd leaned back in his seat and gone right to sleep. Now that he was in Ireland, he was expected to be awake and ready to celebrate Wyatt's wedding festivities.

Mack swallowed a groan. "I'm not here on business or pleasure. I'm here for my brother's wedding."

"A wedding, is it?" The woman smiled and patted his hand on the armrest. "A fine place for a wedding. There's no better place in the world than the Emerald Isle. Their wedding will be truly blessed."

"Sure." Mack didn't have a whole lot of faith in wedded bliss lasting. The odds of most marriages ending in divorce were too high for him to take the leap. He couldn't believe his brother was willing to commit himself to the institution. Mack wondered if he'd knocked her up and felt obligated to marry her. Having been on maneuvers for the past few months, he hadn't had time to talk with Wyatt about his engagement or the upcoming wedding.

Hell, none of his brothers had met the woman. She might not even be right for Wyatt. With him in the army, the chances of this marriage lasting were even slimmer. All the more reason for Mack to make the effort to get there before the wedding. He needed to talk to Wyatt and remind him it wasn't too late to call it off.

"Your brother is a lucky man to have found love in Ireland."

"He didn't actually find his fiancée in Ireland. They met in San Antonio, Texas, in the U.S. I don't know why they decided to have the wedding in Ireland. I think she has relatives here."

"The wedding is in Dublin?"

"As far as I know."

"I met me husband in Dublin when I was a young lass. He swept me off my feet and carried me away to a castle." She stared out at the terminal as the plane rolled to a stop at the gate. "If you have the opportunity to visit Cahir, please, come stay with me in my castle. Me husband and I converted it to a bed-and-breakfast to help with the expense of upkeep. Now that me husband is gone, I manage it mostly by meself. Castle O'Leary B-and-B is its name."

"Thanks, but I think we'll be staying in Dublin the entire time, then I'm headed back to the States." Ah, the States. He planned on taking the full four weeks off, relaxing somewhere on a beach in California near the Marine base. He might even fly out to Texas to his little stretch of heaven in the hill country. The hundred acres of scrub he'd purchased with his signing bonus.

The woman held out her hand. "Me name's Katherine O'Leary, but me friends all call me Kate." She handed him a business card. "If ya ever find yerself in need of a place to stay in Ireland, come to Castle O'Leary. I serve a fine Irish breakfast each morning."

To be nice to the woman, Mack took her card and slipped it into his wallet as the seatbelt sign blinked off. He stood, grabbed his backpack from the overhead bin and stepped out of the way for Kate to stand in the aisle as they waited for the doors to open and the flight to offload.

"Is someone meetin' ya here, or will ya be takin' the train into the city?"

"I'm supposed to have a ride."

"A ride, is it?" She giggled. "Just so you know, in Ireland a ride means sex. It's a lift you'll be wantin'. Well, then, Dia dhuit." Kate smiled and translated. "That's Gaelic for God be with you."

"Thank you," Mack said, not certain how to respond to the older woman who'd just set him straight on sex. "And Dee a dwaht to you," he added awkwardly.

The door opened to the jetway and passengers shuffled out like cattle in a chute. Mack couldn't wait to get his feet on solid earth and a beer in his hand. After thirteen months in an alcohol-free combat zone, he was ready to relax.

As Kate, an Irish national, went one way, Mack joined the long line of foreigners waiting their turn to process through customs. After another forty minutes, he was finally headed toward the door marked Ground Transportation. If his ride—he chuckled—lift wasn't there, he'd hire a rental car and get himself to the hotel.

That's when he remembered...he didn't know what hotel they were staying at. The e-mail he'd gotten from Wyatt had been vague. Fiona's cousin would be waiting for him near the exit for his terminal.

Hell, he'd been in such a hurry to catch his flights he hadn't stopped to ask who Fiona's cousin was or what he looked like. In a terminal full of people coming and going, he could spend a lot of time searching for the cousin.

He stood staring through the exit door and looking back over his shoulder in case he'd walked by the cousin and didn't know it. He felt stupid for not asking for a name or description.

A man walked by carrying a sign with a name on it. Mack started to follow him, until he turned and Mack could read the sign. O'Brien.

He resumed his position near the exit and waited, tired, a little on the grumpy side and ready for that beer.

A woman stepped into the terminal wearing a white, calf-length trench coat, sunglasses and a scarf over her hair. The little bit of legs Mack could see below the coat were trim, smooth, well-defined and gorgeous. He couldn't tell what color hair was beneath the scarf, nor the color of her eyes beneath the sunglasses. The manner in which she carried herself was enough to make Mack look twice. She could be a runway model the way she strode across the floor, one foot in front of the other, the trench coat in no way disguising her tiny waist and slim hips.

A woman like that had to be high-maintenance and completely full of herself, and most likely boring in bed. Basically, an ice princess. Though she was wonderful eye-candy, Mack was not the least interested.

He glanced back at the entrance, wondering when his lift would show up, starting to think he might have to find his own way there.

"Excuse me, sir," a lilting Irish voice said. "What is yer name?"

Mack's insides tightened, and he turned to face the woman with the voice that tugged at something primal.

The ice princess stood in front of him, her full, lush red lips pressed into a thin line. Then she snapped her fingers in his face. "Are you addled?"

"Addled?"

"Do you not speak English?" She stood so close Mack could see several wisps of deep auburn hair sneaking out from beneath the scarf.

He wanted to reach out and yank the scarf from her head and let the dark red hair free. "Yes, I speak English."

"American, eh?" The woman drew herself up on her heels almost but not quite eye-to-eye with him. "Perhaps you could help me. I'm looking for an American named Mack Magnus."

So she was his ride...er, lift. A thrill of annoyance and desire speared through him. Her attitude was beginning to get under his skin along with the desire to pull her into his arms and kiss the lush red lips until he smudged her lipstick.

"Silly name, if you ask me." The ice princess glanced around and back to him, her head dipping as if she was looking him over from head to toe. "You sort of fit the description I was given, but I assumed he'd be a bit more..."

"Handsome?" Mack fought the smile pulling at his lips.

Her brows lifted above the rims of her sunglasses. "The word I was looking for was intelligent."

Mack chuckled. "It just so happens I know Mack Magnus."

"You do? Could you point him out for me?" Again, she looked around at the crowd of people moving in and out of the terminal.

"I could...on one condition."

Her brows disappeared below the edge of the big sunglasses. "Condition?"

He nodded. "Show me your eyes."

Her lips pursed, making Mack want to kiss them even more. "And why should I show you my eyes?"

"I'm curious as to what color they are." He reached up to touch the scarf covering her hair. "Red hair should have green eyes."

She snorted. "My eyes have nothing to do with you or my finding Mr. Magnus."

"I guess you don't want to find this Magnus person." He nodded toward the rush of people. "Go on. Find him yourself."

The woman squared her shoulders and performed an elegant spin worthy of a runway model and marched away.

After a full two minutes of weaving in and out of the crowds gathered around the baggage carousels, she returned.

"Fine. I'll show you my eyes if you'll point out Mack Magnus. Only briefly, because I don't normally take off my sunglasses in public." She turned her head left then right, before removing the sunglasses. "There. Are you happy?" She blinked up at him, her eyes a smoky shade of blue that contrasted brilliantly with her deep auburn hair.

"Beautiful," he said, mesmerized by them.

For a long moment she stared back, the blue of her eyes deepening. Her tongue darted out to swipe a glistening path across her lips and she pressed the hand holding her glasses to her chest. "Are you always this bold?" she whispered.

"Always."

She caught her bottom lip between her teeth and her gazed lowered to his mouth.

He could swear he'd seen those eyes somewhere. Recently. His brows drew together as he tried to remember. "Do I know you?"

She sighed and slid the glasses back on her face. "No. Surely, had I met you before now, I'd remember you for the attractive, yet unfortunately rude and obnoxious, American you are. Now, please point to Mr. Magnus. I have much to do and collecting him is cutting into my time."

"Then you'll be happy to know you've been talking to the man with the silly name all along." He swept a low bow in front of her. "I'm Mack Magnus."

"Jazus, Mary and Joseph." Her smooth tones slipped into an earthier Irish accent and she planted her hands on her hips. "Why didn't you say so in the first place?"

"I would have, but you were on a tear to be as rude and obnoxious as you claimed I was being."

"Jeekers, come with me." She spun on her heels and tripped over Mack's backpack where he'd dropped it on the floor.

He reached out, snagged her hand and yanked her into his arms to keep her from falling flat on her face. The scarf slipped from her head and the sunglasses fell from her face. Her hair tumbled about her shoulders in wild disarray.

Fourteen months in the desert was a long time to go without holding a woman in his arms, a long time without the taste of a woman, without the feel of the soft curves of her body…Mack groaned. The urge to kiss her won and he lowered his lips to hers, claiming them in a searing kiss.

Deirdre Darcy gasped and Mack's tongue swept through the gap between her teeth to caress hers in a long slow glide of wet, sensuous heat. Her fingers curled into his shirt, dragging him closer when she should have pushed the bloody bastard away. Damn him for being so good-looking and cocksure.

When she'd entered the airport, her gaze had found him in an instant. Though she knew plenty of beautiful men through her experiences as a model, she hadn't met one with as much ruggedly masculine charisma as Mack.

As he lifted his lips from hers, he whispered, "Definitely beautiful."

Her heart fluttered and she swayed toward him, wanting a replay of the kiss, not nearly satisfied with just one.

Lights flashed and the click of cameras surrounded them.

"What the hell?" Mack straightened, setting her upright on her feet.

"Feckin' papparazi." Deirdre lifted her scarf up over her hair and snatched her sunglasses from where they'd caught on her sleeve, slipping them over her eyes. "If you want a lift, come with me now."

Before he could take a step toward the door, a woman shoved a microphone in his face. "Sir, are you Deirdre Darcy's lover?"

"I don't know what you're talking about." He pushed the microphone away from his face and matched Deirdre's steps as she exited the terminal.

A man carrying a camera jumped in front of Deirdre, blocking her path. "Ms. Darcy, we understand you're attending a wedding this weekend. Is it yours? Is this man your fiancé?" He snapped several pictures, the flash blinking again and again.

Glad for her sunglasses, Deirdre ignored the question and started around the man. He moved to the side, blocking her yet again. This was exactly the kind of situation she'd hoped to avoid and was dead tired of dealing with.

Mack stepped up beside her and pushed himself between the man with the camera and Deirdre, gripping her elbow in his massive paw. "You're blocking the lady's path."

Much larger than the reporter, Mack towered over him, glaring down his nose like an angry bull.

The man's eyes widened and he stepped aside.

Deirdre marched to the parking garage where she'd left her car, her lips twitching at the way her path cleared with the big American by her side. She could get used to this. Perhaps she should hire a bodyguard when she went out in public. A big one with rock-hard muscles and hands that could hold her like she was lighter than a feather. A guard who could kiss like the feckin' devil himself.

She stumbled. If not for Mack's hand on her arm, she'd have gone headfirst into the side of her car. Straightening, she stared up into Mack's deep-blue eyes and gulped. She swallowed hard before she could get words past her vocal chords. "You can store your bag in the boot." Without waiting for his response, she clicked the button releasing the lock on the lid of the boot.

Mack let go of her arm. "Are you okay?"

"I'll be better once we're out of here." She shook free of his grip, walked around to the right side of the vehicle and slid behind the steering wheel.

Once Mack had stowed his bag and slid into the passenger seat, Deirdre eased the shift into reverse and backed out of the parking space.

"Deirdre Darcy." Mack tapped his finger to his chin and finally shook his head. "Name rings a bell, but I've been too long in the sandbox to remember why. Suppose you enlighten me."

"Sandbox?"

"Afghanistan."

She knew Wyatt's brothers were in the military, but she hadn't stopped to think of where. That they'd been in hostile countries, possibly being shot at, hadn't crossed her mind. Suddenly her status as an internationally known public figure seemed unimportant to the point of trivial. "I guess you could say I'm a celebrity in Ireland."

Once they were out of the parking garage, she pushed the scarf off her head, leaving her sunglasses in place, not ready to reveal her thoughts through her eyes. Every photographer she'd ever worked with had told her that her eyes were the windows to her soul. Every emotion she felt was revealed. For some reason, she didn't want her every thought on display for the handsome man in the seat next to her to see. He was too confident, cocky and annoying by far. And his kiss had left her confused and, for the first time in a decade, needy.

"Celebrity?" He turned toward her. "Actress? Newscaster? No, don't tell me. Weathergirl?"

Deirdre frowned. "None of those." She nodded toward a billboard sign at the side of the highway. "See that sign?"

Mack's glance darted to the sign as they drove past.

In larger-than-life size and brilliant contrasts of dark and light was a woman in a white evening gown with a plunging neckline. She stood in front of a shiny black Mercedes, her deep auburn hair twisted up in an elegant chignon at the back of her head.

Deirdre waited for recognition to dawn.

"Sorry, what was it you wanted me to see? Great car, by the way."

"The woman on the sign. Jazus, Mary and Joseph, you are thick."

"She wasn't bad." Mack shrugged. "A little too highbrow for me."

"You dunce! That's me. Deirdre Darcy. I'm an international model in high demand by every major advertising company in the global market." She glanced at him. He really had no clue who she was. "Oh, that's right, you've been rolling around in the sand for how long?"

"Thirteen months." He winked at her. "I knew it was you. Are you on very many billboards?"

"I've been modeling for nearly a decade."

"Sorry. I'm not much into high fashion. I'm a blue jeans and T-shirt kind of guy when I'm not in uniform."

Why she was letting his sad lack of recognition get to her, she didn't know. Most days she wished for the solitude and anonymity of one who hadn't made a living by having her face plastered over every billboard or television commercial. But Mack's complete disregard for her... Her what?

Self-importance? Her foot left the accelerator as she contemplated her thought. Mack didn't give a kiss of the Blarney Stone for her career or her superstar status. Once she got past her own arrogance, she could appreciate his open honesty. Although he'd been a bit too honest. He'd called her obnoxious. She'd never been obnoxious a day in her life.

Okay, sometimes her red hair got her into trouble. She shook her head to clear her musings. "Which one of Wyatt's brothers are you?"

"I'm the older brother. The other two are younger."

"And all of you are in the U.S. military?"

"We are." He smiled, staring straight ahead as if revisiting a good memory. "Not all of us are in the same branch of the military. Wyatt joined the Army Special Forces. I'm in the Marines. Ronin is a SEAL and Sam is an Army helicopter pilot."

"Are there any more of you?"

"We have a sister. She should be on her way here."

"Is she also in the military?"

"No, she chose to join the U.S. Foreign Services. She works at the embassy in the Ukraine. Much to our father's disappointment."

"Why?"

"She's the baby he always tried to protect. And you know the troubles they're having in Russia now."

Deirdre nodded. "I can understand his hesitation."

"Abby has always had a stubborn streak." Mack smiled. "But she loves her job and she's good at it."

When he talked about his little sister, Mack's smile deepened and he looked more relaxed, less stressed. Positively gorgeous. And gorgeous usually meant one thing. Trouble. "I'm sure if your sister got into trouble, her big brothers would come bail her out, right?"

"Damn right. Speaking of parents...have mine arrived?"

"They settled into the hotel and are getting some rest after their long flight from the States."

"Good. I know Mom will love being here. She always wanted to come to Ireland."

As Deirdre drove through the streets of Dublin, she reflected on how close the Magnus family seemed. A twinge of regret tugged at her. In her global travels following her chosen career, she'd lost the closeness she'd grown up with. The camaraderie of a close-knit Irish family. Sure, she got together on occasion with the rest of her large, extended family, but she didn't have that connection they all seemed to have. Perhaps she'd been away too long.

Fiona had been the one cousin she'd kept in touch with most and she'd grown up in America. Fiona's mother was Irish, Deirdre's aunt, her father had been in the military. She'd been like Deirdre, constantly on the move, never content to stay in one place. When Fiona had informed her she wanted her to be her maid of honor at her wedding in Dublin, Deirdre couldn't say no.

What she hadn't counted on was how much work was involved in the maid of honor position. Though had she known, she still would have accepted. Fiona was a wonderful woman who deserved every happiness.

A little twinge of something akin to envy tweaked beneath the surface as Deirdre made arrangements for the informal wedding at a very old church a friend of the family was able to secure on short notice for the event.

Who knew ordering flowers and arranging for a pianist would spark such a strong tug of longing in herself and a deepening dissatisfaction with her career and the direction her life was heading?

Fiona had been a career woman set in her independent ways when she'd met and fallen in love with Wyatt Magnus. A whirlwind of a romance and three months after they'd met they were scheduled to marry in Ireland and honeymoon in Crete.

Deirdre sighed. Why did some people make falling in love appear so easy? One minute you're happily pursuing your career, the next you're falling all over yourself to please your man.

Fiona's Magnus brother must be as handsome and appealing as the one in Deirdre's car. In that case, Deirdre could understand Fiona wanting to stake her claim before another woman discovered her goldmine of a catch.

"We're staying at the Fitzpatrick Hotel, a four-star hotel close to the church. I believe you'll be comfortable there."

"Sweetheart, I could be comfortable on a stone floor as long as the temperatures don't get above one hundred, no one is shooting at me and sand isn't getting stuck in those really hard to reach cracks. For your information, if we ever go beyond that kiss back there, I can promise you that we won't be making love on a beach. I've had enough sand in my shorts to last a lifetime."

Deirdre's pulse quickened at an image of herself making love with the American on a sandy beach, warm waves washing over their naked bodies. She quickly squelched the image and lifted her chin. "I'll keep that in mind. But for the record, we will never hook up or make love. You're not my type."

He chuckled. The deep rumble in his chest setting her heart to racing. "And what type is that?" he asked.

"I don't know what it is, but I'll make sure you're the first to know when I do."

"Ah, a woman who doesn't know what she wants. Perhaps you haven't been with a man who can show you exactly what it is you need."

She shot him a surprised look. "Cocky much, Yank?"

He shrugged. "Just saying, you haven't been with a real man if you still don't know what you want in the way of sex."

She snorted. "Oh dear, and I suppose you would be the expert to show me?"

"I didn't say that."

"Good. Because I'd have to call you an arrogant braggart."

"I wouldn't want you to sink to name-calling." He grinned and leaned back in the seat. "You have an international image to uphold.

21

Besides, I'm not into high-maintenance women, and you, sweetheart, have high-maintenance written all over you."

She relaxed against her seat, a smile lifting her lips. "You say that like high-maintenance is a bad thing."

"That's right. I'm just here for the weekend and then I'm on to my much-deserved vacation. I only have time and energy enough for a quick fling with the low-maintenance type. No strings attached."

And in a flash, her heartbeat jumped at the American's suggestion of a fling. Not that he wanted one with her. She was high-maintenance, and he wasn't going to be around for long. Then he'd be off to the States for a vacation then back to some far corner of the world to be shot at or worse.

However, if she wanted to have an affair with a gorgeous man, she'd be hard-pressed to find a physical specimen as gorgeous as Mack. It had been over a year since she'd been with a man, and he'd been less than a gentleman, wanting only to be with her because of her status in the fashion industry. How refreshing would it be to make love to a man who only wanted a willing woman, not a leg up in his business?

The weekend was looking to be more interesting by the minute. As with most celebrations in Ireland, the pre-wedding and wedding activities promised to be entertaining.

With a roomful of Magnus brothers, it could be even more entertaining.

"As the best man, am I required to do anything besides stand with my brother and make the first toast to the happily married couple?"

"Seriously?" She glanced his way. "You're the best man. You're supposed to be in charge of the bachelor party, not just going there for a drink."

Mack frowned and sat up. "I forgot about that part. I had really hoped to have a drink and call it a night."

"Hard to believe," Deirdre muttered.

"Seriously, how hard can it be? You know a stripper I can hire on short notice?"

"I do not!" Deirdre exclaimed.

"Well, damn. I'm already falling down on the job. What about a bar where we can go get shit-faced drunk?"

"You won't be pissin' the night away on the eve of my cousin's wedding."

"It's tradition. My brother needs to celebrate his last night as a bachelor."

"And my cousin doesn't need to celebrate her last night as a single woman?"

"Absolutely."

"I'll be sure to line up a stripper for her."

"I thought you didn't know any strippers."

"I only know the male strippers. I assumed you meant female."

He shot a sideways glance her way and winked. "Like I said, you are high-maintenance."

Her belly clenched at that wink and her fingers tightened on the steering wheel. The man had a way of making her body hum with just a look. Feckin' American. "For your information, I've already arranged for the bachelor and bachelorette parties to be held at the Donegal, a small pub in the heart of Dublin. We will have the place to ourselves."

"That won't do at all. The bride and groom need to celebrate separately."

"And they will. The women will be in the back room of the bar and the men will be in the front. Quite separate."

He glanced her way. "You'll be there?"

She lifted her chin. "I'm the maid of honor. I have to be there for my cousin."

"Hmm." His gaze shifted forward. "Save a dance for me, will ya?"

"There'll be little burnin' up the tiles tonight."

"There will be if there's music." He gave her a sexy smile. "Save the dance."

Her knuckles turning white on the steering wheel, she pulled in front of the hotel where they had booked a quarter of the rooms for members of the wedding party. "The pub is within walkin' distance, a block and a half in that direction." She pointed as she turned off the engine and pulled the keys from the ignition. "You'll have just enough time for a shower and to change clothes."

"Is there a dress code?"

She glanced across at him, loving the way he looked in denim. "Something better than jeans will do. Meet me in the lobby in one hour and we'll walk to the pub together. I'd like to be there before the rest of the wedding party to make certain everything is in place."

"Are you sure you weren't a drill sergeant in a previous life?"

"No, but I have four younger cousins I used to keep after school." She slid out of the vehicle, hit the button to unlock the boot and handed the keys to a uniformed valet. She waited for Mack to gather his bag and join her on the sidewalk, before she continued. "I know how to handle bold little boys."

Mack leaned close to her, his lips near her ear. "Just so you know. I'm not a little boy." He kissed the side of her throat, captured the back of her neck and kissed her full on the lips before straightening.

Her heart thundering against her ribs, Deirdre couldn't force a word past her vocal cords. The man was entirely too bold…and big…and sexy as hell.

Then he winked and her knees wobbled.

"See you in an hour," he promised.

Other Titles
by Elle James

Hearts & Heroes Series
Wyatt's War (#1)
Mack's Witness (#2)
Ronin's Return (#3) coming soon
Sam's Surrender (#4) coming soon

Brotherhood Protector Series
Montana SEAL (#1)
Bride Protector SEAL (#2)
Montana D-Force (#3)
Cowboy D-Force (#4)
Montana Ranger (#5)
Montana Dog Soldier (#6)
Montana SEAL Daddy (#7)
Montana Rescue (#8)

Take No Prisoners Series
SEAL's Honor (#1)
SEAL's Ultimate Challenge (#1.5)
SEAL's Desire (#2)
SEAL's Embrace (#3)
SEAL's Obsession (#4)
SEAL's Proposal (#5)
SEAL's Seduction (#6)
SEAL's Defiance (#7)
SEAL's Deception (#8)
SEAL's Deliverance (#9)